A LESSON IN LOVE

Charlotte's friends had warned her about what life as a ballerina would be like. It was a risqué occupation at best for a girl from a wealthy and proper family.

On meeting spoiled and arrogant Sir Richard Shadworth, she learned what real danger there was. Everyone knew of the handsome lord's contempt—and attraction—for dancers. He considered them light-skirts of the most frivolous kind and not to be taken seriously. Until the young beauty taught him that it takes more than genteel breeding to be a lady.

THE
LOVE TANGLE
MAGGIE GLADSTONE

PLAYBOY
PAPERBACKS

CHAPTER ONE

She ought to have been very happy—ecstatic, in fact—
but she was not. She was quite *unhappy,* and for more
than a few reasons. And what was odd was she also
felt guilty because she was not happy.

She had begun as Nancy, the milliner's assistant,
and in a matter of months, something slightly less than
a year, she had succeeded to the style of Miss Faulconer, *première danseuse* of the Italian Opera House.
Except for the fact that she still had much to learn
about the dance, which could come only with some
years of experience, she might have been prima ballerina of the company. Still, for all the lack of years
behind her—she was but twenty—she had caught the
interest of the theatergoing public by achieving that
rare skill of the ballerina, dancing *sur les pointes,* or
toe-dancing, as it was commonly referred to these days.
As far as she knew, she was but the second dancer to
have achieved it—the first in England—and it had
put her above those foreign ladies who practically ruled
English ballet.

Even Madame Fleurette, the Opera's prima balleri-

na, had had to give place to her, but not without a
bit of unpleasantness. However, in the meantime, Lord
Faile, Tony, had switched his allegiance. He had given
up Madame Fleurette and was now paying particular
attention to Nancy. The very fact that this apartment
she resided in was more expensive than even a star
dancer of the ballet could afford attested to the marquis's interest in her, for he it was who had insisted
that she move into it at his expense, the services of
a maid and a cook included. Nevertheless, she had
not been about to allow herself to succeed to *all* the
privileges of his former protégée and, in the face of his
insistence, had tried to make clear to his lordship that
she was her own mistress and no one else's.

Her unhappiness derived, in part, from the fact that
Tony Faile not only was quite handsome and wealthy
but also had always been most encouraging and kind
to her. She had been with him enough to appreciate
the fact that he affected her deeply. The unhappiness
came about because there was only one way for a
marquis and a ballerina to deal together and *that* she
would not have, although she was so sorely tempted,
it caused her physical pain to contemplate it.

The result for her was an ongoing conflict that involved her reason as well as her sensibility. How could
she go on, day after day, in this sumptuous lodging
paid for by his lordship? How could she carry herself
before the world as an independent artiste when it
was common knowledge that she had taken up her
lodging in the very apartment formerly occupied by
Madame Fleurette, who made no fuss over being ac-
claimed Lord Faile's erstwhile light-o-love. Nancy
could not escape it: It was taken for granted that she
was Lord Faile's now.

As she strongly suspected that she was in love with
the marquis, it was no easy thing to meet with him so
very frequently without blushing, and she had to learn

to mask her emotions on more than one count. It was especially necessary as Lord Faile did not make things easy for her. He was ever gentle and gallant with her, never once importuning her for more of her favors than she was willing to bestow. Considering the way of the world in the theater, this was a most unusual circumstance, and it was no wonder that everyone—except, perhaps, her dear friends, her former roommates—believed the worst of her.

Because she made every effort to avoid the intimate with Tony, she could never be sure how his feelings marched with her own. That he was attentive and that there was no gossip to link his name with that of any other female bespoke a certain seriousness in his attention to her, but the difference in their stations defined, almost without exception, the best terms that he and she could come to. It was common knowledge that many years ago the earl of Derby had taken an actress for wife. The very fact that it was common knowledge illustrated clearly how very rare was such a circumstance, and any lady of the theater who dared to aspire to be a marquise must be seven times a fool.

Nancy was quite sure that she did not aspire to that lofty title. She was quite content to be a ballet dancer. Her success upon the stage had been but a dream to her at the beginning. Just to have been accepted into the company was more than she had dared to expect. No, if only Tony had been but a mere gentleman instead of a high noble, she might have been able to entertain such notions to some reasonable degree. As it was, she was sorely tempted to sacrifice everything but her career to be with him, the only reason that she held her career so sacred was that it was all she had. Tony's fickleness with Madame Fleurette was not lost upon her, and she viewed the latter's fate as a sure sign of what a female must be prepared to accept from Tony once his affection waned.

Even beyond that consideration, however, Nancy could not see giving up her career on any account. She had worked too hard for it and had found her success both novel and extremely pleasant. If it had not been for her involvement with Tony, she would have been quite independent, even on her way to becoming as affluent as Mrs. Siddons, the retired queen of the theater. It was a state of being that any female—at least one not born to gentility—must devoutly desire.

The distance that was between Tony and herself was being clearly demonstrated to her this very day. One of the ballerinas was being wed today, and Nancy had not been invited to attend. The reason? It was an affair restricted to gentle folk, and neither by birth nor by vocation could Nancy make any such claim. Yes, it was odd how that had worked out.

When Betsy Medford had come to dance with the company, no one had suspected that she was actually the runaway heiress Sybil Mansfield. Perhaps one could have guessed that it was something like that, for Sybil had been friendly only with Charlotte during her short stay with the Opera, and of them all, Charlotte was the only one to make a claim of gentility. She had been a governess, the only respectable post for a down-at-the-heels lady, until she had figuratively thumbed her nose at the *nice* life and sought out something more interesting, if disreputable, for herself.

Charlotte and Sybil had been rather thick—obviously Sybil had found in her a social peer—and so Charlotte had been invited to the wedding and had gone out on Mr. Westley's arm, an agricultural gentleman who was quite fond of her.

Since Nancy had risen as high as could be expected of her in the theater, she was naturally miffed not to have been invited, especially as she understood that the marquis of Faile would be there. It added fresh punctuation to her dilemma, as if that were needed.

Her great wish to see as much of Lord Faile as she could was bound to be frustrated by this great difference in their respective stations unless she was willing to pay the price of her virtue and her name—no great price at all by the standards of the theater.

Bitterly she recalled that on two occasions she had actually attended the same affair as had Lord Faile, but she had gone as paid performer to dance *en pointe* for the ladies and gentlemen, never as a guest. It had proved most uncomfortable each time—uncomfortable but nevertheless quite pleasant—because Tony had ignored his hostess and devoted himself to her. Still, the episodes had added fuel to the smoldering gossip about them.

She glanced at the tall clock in the corner of her sitting room. In a few hours, Miss Sybil Mansfield would have become Mrs. Geoffrey Chalfont, and with Charlotte and Tony in attendance. Oh, how Nancy longed to have been a part of that, not for any social ambitions of her own, only so that she could be with Tony—on every occasion. But perhaps even if she had been eligible to attend, she would not have been invited. Her position in the company did not permit her to mingle with the ensemble very much, as she had so much more to rehearse than any of them. She never danced in the ensemble anymore. Mr. Coates, manager of the Opera, would not permit it. It would be a waste of her talents, he'd said, and she agreed. It was not so very long ago that she was a member of the ensemble along with Charlotte. It spoke well of the swiftness with which she had acquired a skill far superior to the others in the company, but it only went to make her more alone.

If it were not for Tony, she would never have left Charlotte and Phoebe no matter how far above them in the ballet she rose. And there it was again. Tony was behind all of her dissatisfaction. Things would have been so smooth if it were not for him. Why could he not let her alone!

Immediately she chided herself for the thought. How would she feel now if Tony were to leave her and go off with another ballerina, a true light-skirt this time? It did not bear thinking upon. Her life was devoted to the ballet, but Tony's presence in both made it all so much better. He was a major shareholder in the Italian Opera House, and, if one came to think of it, it would take very little to get him to become a major shareholder in her life.

Oh, Tony, Tony, why could you not have been a ballet dancer, too? You have got the figure for it, and it would have made everything ever so much easier.

Nancy must have been moping along these lines for more than an hour when there came a knock upon the door to the apartment. She was not in a mood to see anybody and called out to her maid to say that she was indisposed.

She heard the door being attended to and then the sound of a conversation. For a moment her pulse raced at the thought that that masculine voice must be Tony's, but reason conquered her excitement. Tony was attending the Chalfont-Mansfield rites. Whoever else it might be, she did not wish to be bothered.

"Indisposed? What, is she ill?"

It *was* Tony! Nancy, without another thought, leaped up and went racing out to him. "Tony, it *is* you," she cried, laughing with glee, unaware that tears were streaming down her cheeks.

"Of course it is me! Are you not ready? What is this? You are weeping!"

Unconsciously Nancy brushed away at her cheek and replied, "Of course I am not. Why ever should you think so?"

The maid, seeing that there was nothing more for her to do, slipped away to chat with cook.

Tony touched her cheek with the tips of his fingers. "I have just come in from outside and I can swear to you it is not raining."

"Oh, it is nothing, nothing at all. I was just feeling a little blue."

"On such a day? I am surprised, or is it that all females must weep at weddings even before they get to 'em?"

"What are you saying? I was not invited to attend Sybil's nuptials. We were not all that close, don't you see."

He frowned. "I cannot see how I came to be mistaken. I know for a fact that Charlotte Lequesne was invited. I had every reason to believe that you would be, too, as you stand so far above her in the ballet."

"It is hardly anything like that, my lord. Sybil and Charlotte were always quite close for the short time that Sybil was with us as Betsy Medford. In any case, I had not the time for her, nor was I all that much taken with her. She is a lady, you know, and so is Charlotte."

The puzzled look in Tony's eyes was replaced by an intent stare as he studied Nancy's delicate features. "You did have a wish to attend, however," he stated, and awaited her response.

"What are wishes? It was unthinkable that I should have been asked. I have no pretensions to such high society."

"So that's it, is it," said Tony heavily. "Come, let us talk."

He took her by the hand and led her into the drawing room. He was quite at home in the apartment. He had spent a great deal of time there, howbeit with another lady.

They sat down opposite each other, and for a mo-

ment there was no conversation between them. Finally
Tony exploded: "Blast!"

Nancy gave a little start.

"I beg your pardon," said Tony. "It is just that this
situation between us, you and me, is becoming most
uncomfortable."

"Yes, I had come to that conclusion myself. I think
that it would be better if I vacated these premises. I am
sure you can find a better use for them, my lord."

"What has come over you, little one? I cannot recall
when I have ever before seen you in this mood. I say,
if it is the wedding, think nothing of it. I have been
invited and they may not deny me my company, especially as she is known to the bride."

"Oh, Tony, how can you say so! If I did not wish to
have some particular party at *my* wedding, I should be
highly wroth with anyone who would dare to contra-
vene my wishes," exclaimed Nancy with great indignation.

"Nancy, my pet, you are making too much of it.
You have said yourself that you did not spend very
much time with Sybil. Your invitation was in all likeli-
hood overlooked, and nothing will be made of the matter if you should elect to appear upon my arm."

Nancy cocked her head and gave Tony a queer
look. "Tony, are you sure that you know what it is
you are saying?"

"I certainly believe so."

"How would you like it if ballet girls made an appearance at *your* wedding?"

"Oh, but this is different, my dear. Can you not see
it? There is Charlotte attending and she is a ballerina,
and the bride herself was a dancer for a time."

"A very short time, and strictly for a lark. It was
not as if she gave herself to the life."

"Well, blast! I wish *you* would give yourself to the
life!"

"I have, Tony. I am devoted to the ballet."

"I wish you would devote yourself to *me,*" he fired back. He was obviously annoyed with her.

Nancy's eyes grew wide as she asked in a little voice, "Am I to repay you, then, for this apartment and all you have done for me?"

"Good God, girl! I never asked you for anything in exchange and I am not doing so now. Is it so painful to you to learn that I would not be averse to something a deal more intimate than what we have between us?"

"Indeed, my lord, it is, because you make me feel beholden to you. It is for that very reason I have got to remove myself from this place. It is yours. Everyone knows it is yours and they all of them think that . . . that . . . You *know* what they think."

Tony was now looking a bit sheepish. "Aye, I daresay I knew how it would be when I gave the place to you. I had hoped that little by little you would get used to the idea and then the fiction would become fact."

Nancy was no longer in a mood to feel sorry for herself. A little flame of anger was stirring within. "My Lord Faile, it is growing past the hour of the ceremony. You will be late for the affair."

"I had been looking forward to it because I thought I would share the occasion with you, but if you are not going, then neither am I."

"I do not see what that will gain you."

He sighed heavily. "If you say so, then neither do I. I suppose that we shall continue on together as usual."

"Tony, you are not making any sense. I am not the only ballerina in the world. I am sure there are many others of us who would give their all to go out with you."

"I say, is that what you think of me? Some overgrown lout who must have his dancing dolls to play with?"

"My lord, I never said anything of the sort."

"You implied it, and do not come this 'my lord' over me. Nancy, you have changed. Why, I can remember when you were but a little mouse of a girl only too delighted to have a compliment from me."

"I shall always be delighted to have a compliment from you, my lord."

"Then I take it you do not dislike me?"

"I like you very much, Tony. You have been exceedingly kind to me and I am forever grateful. I pray you will always be my friend, but we cannot go on in this fashion. I am occupying this lodging to your disadvantage and to my own, for I am very lonely here. I wish to return to Charlotte and Phoebe. I miss them very much. I have never been so alone before."

"I am more than willing to remedy that for you."

"You will allow me to have Charlotte and Phoebe come live with me here?"

His lordship's face fell. For a moment he appeared staggered and only stared at her.

Nancy was baffled by his response and stared back at him, a note of inquiry in her eyes.

Tony pulled himself together and sighed. "Very well, little one, that was not precisely what I had in mind, but if that is what you wish, it is all very well with me. In fact, you do as you damn well please with the place!"

"Have I angered you, Tony?"

"No, pet, not at all. I am just in a bit of a mood with myself. I am not at all sure I know what it is I am doing or trying to do."

"Tony, I should be very pleased to have Charlotte and Phoebe join me if they will, but not if it will put you into a humor. Perhaps I had best move out. I am sure that you have other plans for this place."

"To tell the truth, I *had* plans for this place, but

they seem to have evaporated into thin air. It shall be as I said. The place is yours. Do what you will with it."

"But, Tony, I truly cannot yet afford to maintain it."

"The terms remain unchanged, little one, so you need not fret yourself over it. Now, then, if the matter is settled, come out with me to the park and then we can go to my place for dinner. I know you have a rehearsal tomorrow, so I will not keep you out late."

"But Sybil's wedding——"

"Blast Sybil's wedding and blast Sybil! Somehow she has managed to fill my plate with more than I am in a mood for."

"Are you quite sure it is all right for me to continue on here?" she asked.

"Quite. I pray I may be permitted to call upon you after your friends come to join you?"

"But of course, my lord, it is your apartment. How could I deny you?"

"That is not what I meant, Nancy, and you know it," he snapped.

Nancy, for answer, stood up from her chair and sank into a very theatrical *révérence* before him.

Tony gazed down at her and chuckled. "I cannot say that you are making a new man of me, but certainly a different one. Up on your feet, little one, and let us go for a drive."

CHAPTER TWO

Mr. Arthur Westley lurched his great frame into a more comfortable position so that he might continue to ponder his problem in greater ease. Fortunately for him, his host, who was absent, was built on the same ample plan as himself, with the result that the furniture in the apartment was not unduly restricting to him.

Sir Richard Shadworth, a recognized nonpareil of the sporting world, had given Arthur the liberty of the residence while he was away to Melton country in pursuit of greater excitement than London could afford him. The way things had turned out, however, Arthur was beginning to think he would have been wiser to have gone back to his estate, which was near to Sir Richard's hunting box. It was becoming quite clear to him that while he was an expert in matters of husbandry, sufficient to have repaired his patrimony by this means, he knew next to nothing about London and the females that inhabited the place.

He had come to the City after a life on his farms that had been noted for its utter lack of female companionship. That was almost a year ago. Now he was missing his fields and his crops, beginning to worry lest his people were not maintaining his properties the way he had instructed them to. He was certainly missing any opportunity to garner himself a helpmate, and he was thinking it was because he did not know how to go to work in the business. He had been for too long on the farm.

There was this lovely lady of the ballet he was sure would make him a most excellent wife. She was the most beautiful female he had ever encountered and as poor as he was wealthy. What was more, he had every reason to believe that he was the only gentleman she was seeing. On the face of it, things could not have been more perfect. But there was a problem with the lady, of that he was very certain. More than a few times he had attempted to broach the topic of marriage, only to have her put on a distant air, giving him to feel that she would be quite irked if he attempted to pursue the matter further with her.

He was quite sure that he was in love with her. That his interest persisted in the face of the fact that she plied the trade of ballet girl at the Italian Opera House must speak volumes for the intensity of his passion for her. That she was not cold to him was evidenced by the fact that she was willing to accompany him any time he asked. There never appeared to be anyone else in her life in that regard and, for most of his stay in London, it had been a most encouraging factor for him. Yet time was passing and he had not made any more progress with her.

At first he could not believe his luck. Miss Charlotte Lequesne was by unanimous acclaim *the* beauty of the ballet, and she devoted all the time to him that he could reasonably ask of her. If she had been a light-skirt sort of female, he'd never have given her the least consideration, for all of her great good looks, but she was a lady, both in manner and in fact. Her tale of having been reduced by circumstances to toiling as a governess until she took to the theater to escape the horrors and the embarrassments of that duty was very well vouched for. What could be more perfect?

Now he was at pains to discover, if he could, wherein he had failed to bring her into his arms as his wife after so many months of enjoying her company. He gave vent to a great sigh and shifted his bulk in the armchair once again. He had been going over and over the business for hours and was always winding up confused, hurt, and dissatisfied. He had the greatest need for counsel from a wiser, more experienced head, which was why he had come to London in the first place. Sir Richard was his friend and very much the man-about-town, and Arthur had hoped that Sir Richard could tell him how to bring to an end his bachelorhood in a satisfactory manner.

Shadworth, dying of boredom at the time, had been only too happy to welcome Arthur and show him about the City, but when it came to the female side of London society, Sir Richard had proven useless. He himself was at pains to avoid nuptial entanglements and wanted nothing to do with "high-nosed" ladies. As a result, he had suggested that Arthur get himself a dash of town bronzing and start it by going to the theater, where he would quickly learn who was who in society. Since those were Sir Richard's last words before he had fled from the City, Arthur had little recourse but to accept the advice. That was how he had come to meet with Miss Lequesne.

He knew from the first that she was not in the usual line of the ladies who danced in the Opera, and her manner was so very engaging, on top of everything else he had found to like about her, that his search ended in the Italian Opera House. That was as far as he had got, however, and he could not understand why he could go no further along with her. Richard, who might have been able to tell him, was away in Melton Mowbray, some thirty leagues to the north. If Arthur should decide to go after him, he might just as well give it all up and go home. The trouble with that was that he did not wish to. He had departed his estate firmly resolved not to return without a proper wife. That resolve was shaken now but never abandoned.

There came a banging on the outer door to the lodgings and a voice shouted, "I say, Westley, are you still there?"

A grin split Arthur's features as he leaped from the chair and rushed out to the door far ahead of the man he had engaged to serve him during his stay in town.

He tore the door open and exclaimed, "Dick, old man, how very glad I am to see you! When did you get in? Are you going to be about for a while?"

"You still here?" growled Sir Richard as he came into the apartment followed by his man, whose arms were overloaded with luggage of all descriptions. "Thought you'd have been spliced by this time. You were so hot for the wedded life when I left you. What's happened?"

Arthur frowned. "That's a bloody poor greeting for a friend. If I am in your way, I shall remove myself forthwith."

"And *that's* a bloody nonsensical way to greet a friend. For God's sake, man, have you no compassion? Do you expect a chap to stand about and gab when his throat is as dry as dust? I say, you are not here all by yourself, are you?" demanded Sir Richard, regarding Arthur with an incredulous look.

"No, you simpleton, I hired me a valet. Perkins! Get some brandy in here before you assist Tompkins." He turned to Sir Richard. "Well, what are you waiting for? This is *your* place and *you* are still my host.

Sit yourself down and tell me what it was that has brought you back to town."

Sir Richard dropped into a chair with a groan. "It was the very same damned thing that drove me out to Melton in the first place—boredom! How do you survive up there year in and year out?"

"I have my work. Managing an agricultural estate takes more than a little time."

"But, damn it, outside of a fox or two, there is no company worth mentioning," protested Sir Richard.

"Damn it, it is why I came after you in the first place! A fine host and friend *you* turned out to be. When I needed you most, you were not about. One does not go up to Melton for the sort of company *you* have in mind. I should think you knew that well enough. If you want company, a wife, you have got to go and find her."

"Who in blazes is speaking about a wife? Oh, never mind! There is no use talking to you. I can see that as you are still here, you have not found yourself any sort of company. Why do you stay on, then?"

Perkins came in at that moment and poured the gentlemen their drinks.

"Will there be anything else, sirs?"

"Assist Tompkins any way you can," said Arthur. "And by the way, this gentleman is Sir Richard Shadworth, my host. I think it best that you take your orders from Tompkins until such time as I have something for you to do."

"Very good, sir. Sir Richard, I am honored to find service in the home of so eminent a sportsman." Perkins bowed and left.

Having assuaged his thirst a bit, Sir Richard nodded. "It is nice to know that I have not been forgotten in my absence from this town. Good man that."

"He'd not last twenty minutes at Westley," remarked

Arthur. "Wouldn't know which end of a plow to get behind."

"The man's a valet, not a yeoman. What need has he to know the difference? If you were any sort of proper gent, you'd not be bothered by it, either."

Arthur clapped his hand to his pocket. "And my wallet would be light as a feather, too. Oh, I'll admit that a valet is a handy chap to have about in the city, but where's the need for a blighter like that on the farm?"

"I never suggested there was in the first place, you ass! Now, what have we to do with valets and farms? I want to know what you have accomplished in my absence. Have you met anyone at all?"

"As a matter of fact, I have, and that is what I would speak to you about. I am at point-non-plus with a lady and have not a hint at what I am supposed to do about her."

'Hmmm, sounds interesting. Perhaps I came back at the right time. Tell me about it, old chap."

"She is quite the loveliest creature I have ever laid eyes on, and her name is Charlotte Lequesne."

"Lovely, is she? Odd, the name is not at all familiar to me. I was sure I knew all the beauties in town. Ah, but I am not your man, Westley. I warned you from the start: Leave the ladies alone. Oh, but yes, you have it in mind to wed. Then what, my friend, is the problem? You are very well fixed. I should think that you'd have no problem with the settlements. You are an impressive-looking sort, almost as stout a lad as I am. How can you have any problem?"

"Richard, you go too fast. I have every reason to believe that Miss Lequesne likes me, yet we can never get down to the business of speaking of our futures."

The interest in Sir Richard's face went sour as he remarked, "There! It is as I have always said. It is worth a chap's soul to have to deal with ladies. One has to be pretty desperate to be wed to be able to stand up to 'em."

"Oh, no, Shadworth, I assure you it is nothing like that at all. Charlotte is a most agreeable creature upon every score but that. There is nothing in the least high in the instep about her."

"Truly, Westley, she is at playing cat and mouse with you. I know how it is. They are all alike, these ladies. Pray, where does this charmer reside?"

"In Haymarket on Floral Street."

"Hey? A queer direction for a lady, I should think. There is naught to be found in that district but actors and actresses I should think"

"Oh, perhaps I forgot to mention the fact. She is connected with the theater."

"The theater? A lady? You, my friend, are quite out of your skull," said Sir Richard, bursting into laughter. "Oh, if you are not the greenest of the green!" He caught his breath and continued in the face of a most disapproving look from his honored guest: "It is a very good thing I *did* decide to come home, you bumpkin! It comes of having spent all your time digging rutabagas out of the muck, you benighted idiot! Don't you know that there are no ladies in the theater?"

"Surely you will not deny that Mrs. Siddons is a lady," retorted Arthur, smoldering.

"Oh, well, there is a case of a female, by reason of her great talent, rising above her origins. Still, she is not of the gentry."

"In that case, my Charlotte is above Mrs. Siddons, for she is of the gentry by reason of her birth."

"And she is an actress?" queried Sir Richard, plainly baffled.

"No, she dances in the Opera."

Sir Richard's jaw dropped and he gaped at Arthur. Sadly he shook his head. "Arthur, my dear, dear friend, I see that you are in need of a keeper, and it would appear that fate has selected me for the post. This Charlotte of yours cannot possibly be a lady. Ladies do not dance in the Opera; it is just as simple as that."

"Shadworth, before I am sorely tempted to crack your skull, I think you had better come with me to meet Miss Lequesne so that you may judge for yourself."

"Can you not take my word on it that it is quite an old story? Every young chap goes through this business with a female from the stage. I will admit, however, that it invariably takes place a deal sooner than at your advanced age. Egad, Westley, you ought to be ashamed of yourself for being so callow."

At that point, Arthur got to his feet and advanced toward his host.

Sir Richard chuckled heartily and raised a hand in token of acquiescence. "All right, you noodle, there is no need for us to come to blows over the gel. I tell you what: Give me a day to get my bearings and I shall accompany you to the Opera so that I may meet with this nonpareil and see for myself precisely what it is you have got yourself into."

"That is all I ask," replied Arthur, resuming his seat and smiling.

"But I am not about to go with you unless you understand, here and now, that my judgment of the situation shall be my own, regardless of what you may believe. I mean to say, if I find that it is exactly as I think, then you must accept my opinion or we shall not be friends longer."

"I am perfectly content to let the lady speak for herself, so long as you do not attempt to badger her or show her the slightest disrespect."

"I assure you that whatever I think, my manner will be faultless. I am not a cad, you know."

Arthur nodded his agreement.

Said Sir Richard, "Yes, I must say it is rather good

to be back. It had got quite deadly out Melton way and I am in the mood for an adventure. Come to think of it, I could stand a bit of company myself. I have not made it a practice to find my solace from behind the footlights before this, but it ought to prove interesting."

"I do not see why you look down your nose upon the ladies of the theater. Miss Lequesne was not the only lady in the company. There was another for a short while."

"You don't say! Another of the governess breed?"

"Do not think to make a fool of me. This lady happened to be a recognized heiress—that is, she was incognito while she danced in the company, but she turned out to be, after she had left, none other than a Miss Sybil Mansfield. By this time, I do believe, she is Mrs. Geoffrey Chalfont."

"Mansfield? Chalfont? But these are most respectable names. Are you saying that she was a *ballet girl* and wed Chalfont, the notorious rake? I cannot believe it!"

"It happens to be so. You are not unfamiliar with the names, I see."

"Mansfield is His Majesty's plenipotentiary—or was —and I know that there was a deal of money in his direction. As for Chalfont, I am acquainted with the fellow—nice enough sort but never one to wed, I was certain."

"It just shows that you ought not to shut your mind, Shadworth. I tell you that the ladies of the ballet are not at all what you would have had me believe."

"Egad, I should say not! The Opera has become a blooming Almack's by your account of things. The business gets more interesting with every word. I say, I am beginning to think that my neglect of the ladies of the ballet was most ill-advised. You shall have to bring me up to date, my friend. I would not appear as green as I took *you* to be when we meet with this lady of yours . . . and her friends."

"My pleasure, Dick. Where shall I begin?"

"I say, just let me refresh myself and change. If you are not averse to it, I would suggest that we go out to the Grand Hotel, and over dinner you can tell me all about your adventures at the Opera."

"Do they have a dining room?"

"A superb one, it is called 'The Star' as a token of its excellence."

"Very good. I wish I had known that before. I could have taken Charlotte there."

"I assure you only the very best people dine at The Star," remarked Sir Richard with a grin.

Arthur raised a supercilious eyebrow and replied, "Precisely why I would wish to entertain Miss Lequesne there, old chap."

CHAPTER THREE

Charlotte came into the large garret on Floral Street that she shared with Phoebe Bell and exclaimed, "I swear, Phoebe, it has got beyond anything. Bouquin was particularly beastly today. There was not a thing we did that he did not find something to remark about. And, if you know the signor, you know how nasty he can be. Today he was particularly abominable. Nothing would suit. Over and over again we had to dance the same piece. You are so lucky to be out of it."

Phoebe grinned. "My dear, that is not news to me. Considering my dancing ability, I am thrice-blessed to remain a member of the company and I am well aware of it. I will admit I found it quite a bore at the beginning, having to stand about like a statue for hours on end, but when I saw the hard work that you poor things were put to and for the same wages as myself, I said, 'Phoebe, this is a deal better than peddling fish, so make the best of it,' which I did."

Charlotte let out a groan and fell into a chair. "Your view of things is not at all calculated to soothe my aching feet." She bent over and began to massage her feet, having slipped out of her shoes. "I really do not think that I care to go on with this business of ballet. I mean to say, where does it lead a girl?"

"Nancy is doing quite all right, I should say. She seems to have arrived."

"I daresay you are referring to Lord Faile?"

"But of course. The little one has done very well for herself, better than *I* have done by far, I'll take my oath."

Charlotte shook her head in disagreement. "I am not so sure. Nancy does not have the appearance of a girl who has achieved what she wanted. I think she is looking a bit worn of late."

"The child does not know when she has had enough. She is working too hard, much too hard," said Phoebe. "I mean to say, she cannot expect to go on with her toe-dancing, *and* all the rest, with Lord Faile demanding so much of her time."

"Phoebe, whatever you are thinking, you are out in it. Nancy swears that she and Lord Faile are just friends, nothing more."

"I should love to have such a friend. Even I have not yet been able to find so attractive a sponsor willing to grant me carte blanche."

"Oh, I do not believe that," replied Charlotte. "The way you have been carrying on with every Tom, Dick, and Harry in the lobby, you could have had as much as Nancy, if not more. Actually, I am quite surprised that you have not taken up with a gentleman before this. Are you become so particular?"

"Perhaps," said Phoebe vaguely. "It was quite a change from Billingsgate at the beginning. Phoebe Bell to be thick with noble dukes and earls—it was quite a thing for me then. Now I am not so sure I care for what is forever on their minds. I mean to say, there is nothing the least romantic about those gentlemen. I thank my stars I am blessed with a bit more strength than any of them suspects. That is one thing hauling about hundredweights of fish gave to me. I never thought I would be thankful for it. Bah, when you come down to it, all of them are puny except for Lord Faile, but, of course, he is spoken for."

"I wonder. Madame Fleurette is certainly out of his consideration and Nancy *may* be the one, but I do not think so. She will not admit to it, at least."

"I say, do you think she can be ashamed of it?" queried Phoebe.

Charlotte shook her head. "No, I do not think it is that. I think she is troubled about it, and if that is it, then, I warrant you, there is something still to occur between them."

"Oh, I cannot believe it is so!" expostulated Phoebe. "He has given her an apartment, very sumptuous, according to Fleurette's account—and she ought to know, as it was hers formerly. I cannot be convinced that Lord Faile or any of his ilk would give a girl so much and expect nothing in return."

"I am not saying what his lordship expects, my dear. I am only implying that he has received no favors from Nancy other than his company, and that on a most unexceptional basis."

"Nonsense! I have been with the best of them and I know," replied Phoebe most emphatically.

"Phoebe, I do not hold any great brief for the gentlemen who haunt the lobby, but I, too, can speak from experience, and I know it is quite possible for a gentleman to make that sort of offer out of tender regard."

"Charlotte, I took you for being more up to snuff than that," said Phoebe disdainfully.

"I tell you it is true. I *know* such a gentleman."

"That chap Westley?"

"Precisely so. Mr. Westley would do anything for me and has said as much. I have no doubt that a fine lodging for me would be quite within his province."

"Then why are you still here?" demanded Phoebe.

"I have an affection for Mr. Westley but not in that way. In any case, I am not about to indulge in that sort of thing. I still have a very serious hope of finding me a worthy gentleman to have me for wife."

"Silly, childish nonsense!" exclaimed Phoebe, shaking her head. "That is the dream of every ballet girl, and I have yet to hear of one who had it come true."

"There was the Countess Derby——"

"Yes, I have heard all about her. First of all, she was an actress and could act the lady."

"I beg your pardon! I do not have to act the part; I *am* a lady."

"Now, Charlotte, I am not saying that you are not. It is just that in the eyes of the world you are a ballet girl, and we ballet girls are not considered to be in the best odor. You had better face it, my dear. All I am saying is that if this chap Westley is hot for you, you ought to make the most of it."

"Oh, leave him out of it, I pray. I am not in a mood for this discussion."

"You are continuing to see him, are you not?"

"Naturally. He is the only gentleman friend I have got."

"That is only because you are so particular, my dear. Truly, Charlotte, sometimes I have the feeling that you are not blessed with a bit more bronze than Nancy."

"Well, I think that Nancy is suffering from the very reason that I have refused all overtures from Mr. Westley."

"I do not understand you. What do you mean?"

"Simply that by accepting this apartment from Lord Faile, she has put herself under an obligation to his lordship. Even if he does not press the point, still Nancy is very sensible of it, and it must make her uncomfortable if she is not prepared to accept him as her lover, to put it bluntly."

Phoebe looked shocked. "Charlotte, what are you saying? I never thought I should live to see the day when *you* would allow such an unmaidenly sentiment to cross your lips."

Charlotte smiled. "It is high time, don't you think? If you think being a ballerina is so bad, never try for a governess, my dear. That is *not* a life for a lady, I assure you."

Phoebe chuckled. "Not a beauty like you, I am sure."

Charlotte cocked her head. "Come, Phoebe, you are not so behind hand when it comes to making a lovely appearance. How have *you* managed?"

Phoebe, very ungracefully, brought up her hand and balled it into a fist that was rather impressive for one of the fair sex. "This, my pet, I have never hesitated to use. You see, that is one of the advantages of not being born and bred a lady. The gentlemen know that I will use it if they press me."

Charlotte chortled. "Indeed, I can believe it."

There was a knock on the door at that moment and both ladies jumped up.

"Oh, dear—visitors," said Charlotte, primping at her hair. "I am sure I look a sight, and I truly am not in any mood. Who can it be, do you think?"

A voice called out. It was light in tone, definitely that of a young female. "Charlotte, Phoebe . . . may I come in?"

"Why, it's Nancy!" they exclaimed together, and made a rush for the door.

The affectionate greeting the two ladies gave to their young friend was rather surprising, considering not only that they saw her every day at rehearsal but also that Nancy, their erstwhile roommate, had far surpassed them in the company, although all three women had received their appointments to the Opera House on the same day. However, there was not a trace of envy in the greetings that Charlotte and Phoebe bestowed upon Nancy. They were truly glad to receive her.

They drew her into the room without ceremony and plumped her down upon the bed that used to be hers. Charlotte was bursting with questions: "Little one, it is so good to see you to talk with. We never have a chance to do so at work anymore. I was beginning to think that you had become too grand for us."

"Oh, never, sweet Charlotte! It is a fact that I have missed you both, and that is why I have come."

"I was sure that we would have had a chance to converse at Sybil's wedding." Charlotte said. "It was a grand affair. Almost everyone was there. Why were you not?"

"I was not invited."

"Oh, but surely that cannot be!" exclaimed Charlotte. "I cannot believe that Sybil could invite me, a mere ballerina, and not you, *première danseuse* of the Opera. Perhaps your invitation was misdirected."

"I do not think so. Were you invited, Phoebe?"

"Now, of course that was not to be expected. Sybil turned out to be a grand lady. What has a girl from Billingsgate to do with such a one as she?" Phoebe replied.

"By the same token, Phoebe, what has a former milliner's assistant to do with the likes of Sybil?" said Nancy.

"Oh, but that is in the past, my pet," Charlotte pointed out. "I am sure that there was some error."

"Not by half, Charlotte. You are a lady, and Sybil was always willing to accept that fact. She did not forget and there was no error. To the best of my knowledge, no one but you of the company was invited."

"Oh, dear, if I had known, I should not have attended. It is almost a cut direct," said Charlotte, quite put out.

"I should have liked to have seen what it was like. I have never been a part of a grand social function. I have entertained at a few—and Lord Faile was always about to see that no embarrassment was offered me— but, of course, it is not the same as being a guest."

Charlotte's brow furrowed. "Come to think of it, his lordship did not make an appearance either. Sybil was quite put out about it."

Nancy's lips spread in a crooked grin. "Aye, I know about that."

"It was because of *you*," said Charlotte.

"Hip, hip, hooray for the little one!" piped up Phoebe. "You have got him in your pocket. I thought as much."

Nancy blushed. "Oh, no, Phoebe, it is nothing like that, I do assure you. It was only that his lordship appreciated that I was disappointed and went to work to console me."

"You have got him in your pocket," Phoebe repeated with a judicial nod.

"I tell you not!" insisted Nancy. "It is just that Lord Faile and I have an understanding——"

Phoebe laughed coarsely.

"Oh, Phoebe, I do wish you would let me finish!" snapped Nancy.

"Look you, little one, I am quite fly to every game these gentlemen play. I tell you, you have got the marquis in your pocket, and I say more power to you. I thought I was up to the nines on all counts, but I must give place to you. Naught to be ashamed of, pet. Faile is quite a catch on any terms. There are few to match him in wealth even if they might match him in title, and for appearance, his is not to be sneezed at, wouldn't you say, Charlotte?"

"I tell you it is not like that at all. Tony and I are dear friends——"

" 'Dear friends'!" interrupted Charlotte. "Nancy dear, one cannot be just 'dear friends' with so exalted a gentleman. Even with the advantage of *my* breeding, *I* could not expect that."

"I tell you it is so!" insisted Nancy, close to tears. "He is very fond of the way I dance."

Charlotte frowned. "I admit I did wonder how it was between you. Still, my dear, I must warn you to step carefully."

"Nonsense!" said Phoebe. "Tell me, pet, is he in love with you?"

"Surely not," replied Nancy, almost aggressively. "What a thing to bring up. Lord Faile is an unexceptional gentleman in every way. He is kind and considerate and *friendly*."

"Then pray tell us—your dear friends, pet—are you in love with him?"

Nancy was too quick to shake her head. The blush that reddened her cheeks contradicted her action, and as she did not trust herself to speak, she ended up in rosy confusion.

There was a mournful look in Phoebe's eyes as she gazed at her diminutive friend.

"This is not good," said Charlotte. "I must suggest that you leave that apartment of his and come live with us. To stay there will only break your heart. Sooner or later he is bound to tumble to it and take advantage of you, my dear."

"Oh, but he has not a clue, I assure you. In fact, that is why I have come to call. It is quite lonely there and I would have you join me. After all, we did share this garret together. Now that I have managed to have a bit of good fortune, I have a wish to share it with you both."

"Oh, Nancy, it is so kind of you. I am sure I shall

never forget that you made the offer, but we must face the obvious. I am not so sure about Phoebe, but I could never afford such a grand place."

"It is outside of the question, Charlotte. The place is Faile's, I do believe," said Phoebe, "and it is beyond reason to expect that he would stand still a minute while you and I took up our lodgings with Nancy there."

Nancy offered, "It is true he was not particularly enthusiastic about the idea when I made the suggestion, but he did not deny me."

Both Charlotte and Phoebe turned to stare at Nancy. Nancy, understanding their shock for doubt, said, "I assure you it is as I said. You see, I complained to my lord about the solitude and wished to depart, but he would not have it. That is when I asked to be allowed to have you join me."

"He . . . he had no other suggestion to make?" asked Phoebe, eyeing Nancy intently.

Again Nancy's cheeks deepened in color. She bit her lip, then laughed and said, "Well, yes he did, but I did not understand what he was driving at at the time. I daresay I should have been terribly embarrassed if I had. But he *did* give the place to me."

"Oh, Nancy, you may not keep it," said Charlotte. "It is well beyond your means and ours, too, into the bargain. I know how much apartments rent for in that district."

"But that is the beauty of it, don't you see. Actually it will be a saving, for his lordship will maintain the lease and the maid and the cook." She paused and brought a finger up to her cheek as she pondered a point. "You know, I do believe that we could use at least one additional maid for us, perhaps two. I had better let Tony know about it."

Charlotte opened her mouth to protest, but Phoebe stretched her hand out to take hold of Charlotte's arm.

Giving it a little shake to quiet her, she said, "You do whatever you think is best, little one. If you want us to come live with you, I should dearly love to."

Charlotte turned to stare at Phoebe, a great question in her eyes. Phoebe gave her a meaningful look in which there was the slightest hint of "Don't you dare!"

Charlotte gave a little shrug of helplessness and said, "Indeed, Nancy, I am sure I should be delighted if the three of us could pick up the threads together once more. I have missed not having you about, and in this way I am sure I should not be at worrying about you so much."

"Marvelous!" cried Nancy, all smiling. "Now I must go to inform Lord Faile of our new arrangement and ask that he engage us some more servants." With that, she gave a hug and a kiss to each of her friends and tripped gracefully out of the chamber.

Charlotte turned to Phoebe. "What do you make of all of this? I am sure I never heard the like."

"It is obvious to me. They are in love with each other. It stands to reason, else it were all the most ridiculous nonsense."

"Oh, but you are being over-romantical, Phoebe. I am surprised at you."

"Dear Charlotte, you were ever the one to worship true romance, and now, when it buds beneath your eyes, you do not see it. I am merely a rough customer out of Billingsgate, not at all inclined to this romance foolishness, so it is surprising, to say the least, that I recognize what you do not and should. Lord Faile and Nancy are in love with each other, but they are so far apart in station that they cannot see it for what it is."

"But that could be rather dreadful for Nancy."

"Aye, it could. That is why I think it a most excellent idea that we go to be with her. I'll wager that if his lordship were not in love with our little friend, he would never stand for two perfect strangers being added to his pension rolls."

"What a horrid thing to say! We are *never* his lordship's pensioners."

"Call it what you will, he shall be keeping us as much as though we were a deal more to him than we are actually."

Charlotte frowned in indignation. "Heavens, it is all about that Nancy is his paramour now. What will be said of *us* if we become a part of that ménage?"

"It will certainly serve to puzzle most. Whatever is said, you may safely bet that it will never be said to his lordship."

"I am not about to add fuel to the fire. I have my good name to defend."

"There you go, being all-over missish again. You have got to go. You have no choice, now that Nancy needs us—and, I tell you, she needs us more than she knows."

Charlotte knit her brows in puzzlement. "Phoebe, I am not at all clear as to what you are trying to say."

"My stars, but I never thought I should be called upon to explain things to a lady! Can you not see what might happen between them?"

"Yes, of course. In this business it is one of the hazards of being a ballerina. I assure you I have tried to forewarn Nancy about just such a situation. If you will recall, when first we began together in the theater, I made it a point to keep Nancy away from the lobby for just that reason."

"Aye, and the little minx put all your trouble to naught by walking off with the greatest prize of all and against all odds. I admire her for it, but I side with you. It is not the thing for Nancy."

"I assure you it is not the thing for me, either!" said Charlotte angrily.

"Just between you and me and the gatepost, my

lady, it is not my cup of tea, either," said Phoebe, much to Charlotte's surprise.

Charlotte gasped. "Oh, Phoebe, how can you say so? I am sure that you have one affair after another. I truly believe that was the only reason you came to try out for the ballet in the first place. I do recall that your pockets were loaded, whereas Nancy's and mine were to let, and if it were not for your generosity at the time, we would never have found a place to lay our weary heads."

"You are quite out in your thinking, my dear. I came to the trials because I had a wish to do something better with myself than peddle fish the rest of my life, and true, once I witnessed what went on in the lobby, I took a hand in the game, but I was not so silly as to go in and lose my all. Just because I am a Billingsgate girl is not to say that I was bred to be a light-skirt. We Billingsgate ladies are not all that free with our favors, and there's many a fishing cove who regretted the day he laid hands on Phoebe Bell without being asked."

"B-but I *saw* you. I saw how you went on with the gentlemen——"

Phoebe laughed. "Those hot-blooded bucks fell all over themselves to get at me, and I let them tussle with each other for the privilege. Why, my darling, your head would swim at some of the offers that were made to me. But if I had accepted even one of them, do you think I should still be sharing this garret with you?"

Charlotte was in tears now. "Oh, Phoebe, I have been dreadfully unjust to you in my opinions. I am so ashamed."

"Bah! You take these things too seriously. I daresay that is how it is with the gentry. You could have a deal more fun if you managed to see things my way, but then you are a lady and there's an end to it."

Charlotte rushed over to Phoebe, putting out her

hand. "My dear, I shall never forgive myself for having thought so ill of you."

Phoebe took hold of her hand and gave it a squeeze. "Do not fret so, my dear, or you will have me in tears in another moment. Come, we have a deal to do if we expect to rest our heads on a West End bed this night."

It took Charlotte aback. "So soon? What if Nancy cannot gain his lordship's approval?"

"Then it will be so much harder for him, for we shall already be there, don't you see. In any case, I imagine Nancy could ask the world of him and get it, too. Let us not delay. I have heard it said that possession is nine points of the law, and Nancy needs us, the poor darling. I should like to get a better look at Lord Faile than it has been my privilege till now."

"I feel very uneasy about it all," protested Charlotte.

"So do I, that is why we had best be on our way."

"Phoebe, you positively amaze me. Nothing stops you, not even the prospect of a marquis's anger."

Phoebe laughed. "After all, what can he do about it? The trouble with you, sweet, is that at birth *you* got all the breeding, whereas *I* got all the brains, I am thinking."

CHAPTER FOUR

The hackney carriage went along at a leisurely pace down Oxford Street on its way toward Haymarket. Within, two gentlemen, very much at ease, were engaged in conversation.

Arthur Westley was speaking very earnestly: "Shadworth, I do not understand your attitude. Just because a female is reduced by circumstances to earning her living in the Opera is no reason to condemn her. I mean to say, Charlotte would be a lady no matter what the circumstances."

"My dear Westley, I could wish you would stop singing that same song. I have already agreed to come along with you. You have agreed that I shall be free to consult my own opinion with regard to this Miss Lequesne of yours. What more would you have?"

"Simply this: I would have your opinion uncolored by your attitude, which I find reprehensible to a degree. You are prejudging the lady and you have never laid eyes upon her."

"I assure you, dear chap, I am not prejudging the lady in question. I have only given voice to a remark that ladies, *true* ladies, are not to be found in the ranks of a ballet troupe. I have never heard of one so and I do not, at this late stage, expect to find one so. That is all I have said."

"And that is more than enough. It is as I have said: You are prejudging the case."

"And I insist that I am not. I am merely taking into account the circumstances under which we shall discover this 'lady' of yours. I mean to say, at least if she had been a singer . . . now, they are almost respectable. The only thing one can say against them is that they are a brazen bunch to show themselves off in public. But a dancer? An Opera dancer? Why, they appear practically unclothed as they prance about on the boards. How would you feel to know that the woman who is to be the mother of your children had made a spectacle of herself before all the bucks of London?"

"You are not at all kind to bring that point up, Richard," remarked Arthur, a certain look of anxiety filling his eyes.

"I am not trying to be kind at this moment; I am trying to be a friend to you, Westley. You will think me the personification of kindness another time, when you have lost that green-as-grass air about you."

"If you are bound to condemn her, why come with me in the first place?" snapped Arthur, falling back in his seat, defeated.

"I have a bone of curiosity to see a female who can put on the airs of a lady when she is engaged in such a debased occupation."

"You make me sick to death. I feel as though I am throwing Charlotte to the lions by bringing *you* along."

"It is never as bad as all that. I assure you I shall not cause you any grief with her. I know how these things are, my friend. You may rely upon me to be everything that is gallant. Frankly, I have never had a taste for the Opera, and so perhaps it is a good thing that I am joining you this evening. Everything else has palled, and I am in need of something different in the way of entertainment at the moment."

"Your motives are less than complimentary. I pray your intentions are in better form."

Sir Richard snorted. "Bah! Westley, you ought to have stayed away in Leicestershire. I do not think that London is at all the place for you. You take everything much too seriously. You ought to sit back and take advantage of every little bit of adventure that comes your way. Lord knows you have not done anything like this in your lifetime, and if you return to your mucky turnips before you have given yourself the chance, I'll wager it will be a mangold you will bed and never a wife."

"I could wish you had stayed in Melton," was all the reply Arthur could muster. He relapsed into a brooding silence as the cab continued on its way through the evening.

When the English theatergoer put down his pair of shillings, be he drama fancier or opera lover, he expected to be entertained to repletion. And so it was that London theater managers were forever at pains to fill out an evening for their patronage. This invariably called for presenting more than one work in an evening, and in the past, at the beginning of the century, as many as three or four would be given; a play, a pageant, and a farce was a usual combination. Perhaps to pad the bill, as well as to make up for the lack of great talent, works were altered drastically and shortened dreadfully in order to fit them into the evening's entertainment.

However, even if slowly, times had changed, and theater managers were now called upon to make more sophisticated and artful presentations. The Kemble family had much to do with that, having brought to theater management and to the art of acting a new, higher standard. Although the great Mrs. Siddons, sister of the eminent actor/manager John Kemble, was in retirement, the impress of her taste and talent had permeated the British theater and elevated the tastes of her devotees, who were legion.

For the Italian Opera House in Haymarket, this maturing audience was something of a strain, especially for Mr. Coates, its manager. He had not only mere playactors to contend with but also singers, dancers, and musicians, and the varying temperaments, all fragile to a degree, caused him many a sleepless night.

Mr. Coates's ballet master, Signor Bouquin, was by far the most difficult of his people. The signor, a Frenchman trained in the Italian School of ballet, was forever making demands upon Mr. Coates that the manager was hard put to meet. Money, of course, was one of the strains. The other, which for the longest time could not be got over, was talent. It was not that English ballet dancers were hard to find; rather, it was that talented ones were almost nonexistent. And so, when it was discovered that Miss Faulconer, *"la petite"* not only was English but also could dance quite well indeed, both Mr. Coates and Signor Bouquin were overjoyed. What was more, Miss Faulconer had learned to dance *sur les pointes* practically all by herself, and that had filled their cups to overflowing. It also brought another problem along with it, howsomever. The prima ballerina of the company, Madame Fleurette, a genuine French dancer of unchallenged grace, had no wish to be displaced by anyone, much less a green girl, English or otherwise. There had been a bit of a fuss when Nancy was being brought forward, but a sort of peace had settled upon the company when it became clear to Madame Fleurette that she had lost Lord

Faile's interest. Although she had managed quickly enough to find herself another sponsor, Lord Faile's defection had stripped the lead ballerina of her influential connection, and she had to rest content with what she had left—the most remarkable talent for the dance in the land. Perhaps, if her toes had been something less tender so that she could have mastered the art of toe-dancing, Miss Faulconer would never have grown to be such a challenge to her. It was no reflection on Madame Fleurette's ability. Dancing *en pointe* was a ballet master's dream that was just coming true at the time. For the moment, Nancy Faulconer was the first practitioner of the art in England, and there were not many others in the world who had achieved it.

The uneasy peace came to an end when Signor Bouquin announced that he was about to realize his own particular dream. In the year 1808 at the Opéra, Paris, he had danced the part of Antony in Jean Pierre Aumer's *Les Amours d'Antoine et de Cléopâtre.* Now, for the privilege of putting on the work himself, he was prepared to come out of his retirement and dance the part of Caesar, yielding Antony's role to the *premier danseur,* the much younger John Clack. And for Cleopatra, he could not see anyone other than Nancy in the part. This left Madame Fleurette with the role of Cleopatra's maid, Iras, which was nothing less than an insult, as she let both Bouquin and Coates know in no uncertain terms.

The rehearsals that ensued were more in the nature of civil wars, and a final peace was achieved only when Signor Bouquin, with a distaste amounting to revulsion, agreed to enlarge the part of Iras out of all context so that Fleurette would have as much to do in the ballet as did Nancy. Once that had been settled and the revisions incorporated into the piece, the rehearsals went along with their usual confusion but a deal less rancor.

It was this work that Sir Richard and Arthur were to witness this night.

As the piece was not long enough to meet the needs of the audience, it was preceded by that perennial favorite, Mozart's *Figaro,* shortened for the occasion. Since neither Sir Richard nor Arthur had come to the theater for the singing or the music, they spent most of that part of the presentation out in the lobby, consorting with other gentlemen of similar tastes.

Finally, the opening number found them in the Shadworth box, all eyes upon the stage. The music began and the curtains parted.

Sir Richard having no acquaintance with any of the ballet company, it fell to Arthur to point out who was who upon the stage in response to his inquiries. Arthur was satisfied to have named only Charlotte, but Sir Richard was not until he had had all of the principals pointed out to him, particularly the tall, amply-endowed female who, although she never danced a step, stood about rather gracefully in quite a few scenes for no apparent reason. That her attire was more scant than the other ladies' raised no objection with anyone, and when she came onstage carrying a bow and wearing a quiver of arrows, a Greek Diana misguided into the midst of Egypt, still no one objected, least of all Sir Richard.

"Gad," he breathed, his eyes glued upon her person to the exclusion of all else upon the stage, "I should like to see her on a horse!"

"Charlotte?" asked Arthur.

"No, that other—Miss Bell, did you say?"

"Oh, Phoebe. She cannot dance a step."

"She does not have to, for my money," replied Sir Richard, quite entranced. "I say, what do you know about her?"

At the moment, as the ensemble was onstage, Arthur had no wish to be distracted from his rapture by idle conversation.

"Later, old chap, later," murmured Arthur, his eyes following the figure of Charlotte, and only Charlotte, through every turn.

"Come, out with it, friend. Don't be an old screw."

Arthur turned, in a high state of exasperation. "Damn you, watch the bloody show and leave me be! Later, I tell you!"

People in the other boxes started to stare, some of them bringing their glasses up to their eyes and frowning at them.

"Now see what you are doing," said Sir Richard. "Stop making such a fuss and speak."

"Hush!" "Shhh!" came from all sides, and Arthur was quite defeated. He stood up, grabbed Sir Richard by the arm, and dragged him unceremoniously out of the box into the corridor. Without releasing his hold upon him, he marched him back to the mezzanine, which was quite deserted.

"Blast your eyes, Shadworth, that was a miserable performance you gave back there! Had you a wish to disrupt the ballet, you could not have done it better."

Sir Richard was grinning as he slowly disengaged Arthur's hand from his arm. "Blast *your* eyes, Westley, but I had to speak with you, and I was sure that we could not hold the conversation that I had in mind in the box or we should truly have disrupted the show. Now, be a good chap and tell me about Miss Phoebe. She is a miss, I pray, although I'd not let that get in my way with her."

"You have no appreciation of the finer things, you lump!"

"On the contrary, I have every bit as much as you do. I saw the lady who has got you in her pocket and, indeed, I can understand your devotion to the ballet. I am suddenly taken with a similar interest and have every intention of devoting myself to a serious study of the art. Now, then, tell me about Miss Bell."

"Could it not wait? I am missing Charlotte's entire performance."

"You are only wasting time with your complaints. I am not about to let you off before you have told me what I wish to know. Believe me, you have dragged me out here and I intend to keep you here. By George, but I have been wasting my time in Melton when all the time you have had this garden of roses to play about in. You could have at least written to me of what you had discovered."

"You did not care for ballet. If you will recall, they were just about your last sentiments to me before you left."

"All right, I have changed my mind. Let us not stand about debating the wonder of it, but do you tell me about Phoebe Bell. I have a very strong wish to begin an acquaintance with her."

"Then you shall have to go to the end of the line, old man. There are gentlemen of the highest degree hoping for a share of her company."

"The highest?"

"The very highest. Dukes—at least, there is Belgrave paying her all sorts of attention."

Sir Richard's face fell. "It begins to appear that she is too rich for my blood. Why does she continue on in the ballet if she does so well for herself?"

"She is a strange sort of girl. Oh, she is very likable, most good-natured, but rather independent for one of her antecedents and vocation. I mean to say, she is not a lady like Charlotte, you will understand."

"You speak as though you are more than merely acquainted with her."

"Well, I ought to. She is Charlotte's roommate. They share the same shameful lodging, a garret on Floral Street."

"Ah, yes, I believe you said as much before; but that is indeed strange. From what you say, she could have the finest apartment in London. I know *I* would be quite willing to set her up."

"Yes, you and all the gentlemen of London."

"But you are acquainted with her. It should present no problem, then, to arrange an introduction. When is this blasted show over? You can present me to her this very evening."

"No, not this evening. Charlotte has indicated that she would be too fatigued to go out after this performance, and so I shall not be seeing her until tomorrow. The ladies will have the day off, you see."

"That suits me to a tee. Tomorrow it is."

"But, Shadworth, I had better warn you. Miss Bell is considered extremely fast."

Sir Richard laughed. "And so am I. What are her other good points?"

"She hails from Billingsgate, where she was bred to be a fishwife."

For a moment Sir Richard looked stunned, then a broad grin spread over his countenance. "Yes, I'll wager she was. Bah! I would not believe it even if it were true. That fine figure of a female out of Billingsgate? Not on my life!"

"I'll not debate the point. It is common gossip."

"Devil take the gossip! I'll take Miss Phoebe, Billingsgate or no."

"Oh, but I say!" exclaimed Arthur, something put out. "You were supposed to help me with Charlotte, and here you have gone and put it completely out of your mind for Miss Bell."

"You have to admit that she can put a chap's mind into fair pastures; but never despair, old thing. We can kill two birds with one stone. Why do you not invite Miss Lequesne out and have her ask Miss Bell to join her? In that way we can get all our business done."

Arthur nodded. "That might not be a bad idea. I'll send her a note the first thing tomorrow. Now, if you are satisfied, perhaps we may rejoin the audience and see what is left of the performance."

"A jolly good idea!"

CHAPTER FIVE

Charlotte came into the new apartment on Great Pulteney Street, close by Golden Square, and rid herself of the packages filling her arms. She let them slide onto a table in the entranceway and reached for the little watch on her neck ribbon. It was of gold, and the Lequesne coat of arms was engraved upon its finely polished cover.

"Good heavens, I had not thought it would take so much time!" she exclaimed, and went sailing through the apartment, calling out for Nancy and Phoebe. All she managed to rouse was Bridget, the new maid, who informed her that her other mistresses had not returned from the shops.

Charlotte instructed her to place the packages in her room and then wait upon her as she changed for the evening. She was feeling rather fatigued. A day spent shopping could be ever so much more exhausting than giving the great performance of last evening. She had taken much too long to accomplish it and must now be late for her appointment with Arthur. She would have to rush if she was to be even near to ready when he called for her. She had not seen him for the past few days, at her own request. The Cleopatra ballet had called for more skill in the dance than most of the other pieces the corps had had to do, and she had not been in a mood to be charming. Arthur had been very sweet, he had understood. It gave her a little twinge to think of him. She liked him immensely, but that was all. She would never wish to lose him as a friend; however, she could not see in him the man of her dreams.

She had not been at her toilet for very long when the sound of her companions entering the apartment came to her ears. She interrupted her dressing long enough to don a wrapper and go out to greet them.

As usual, Phoebe was filled with hearty good cheer, and Nancy obviously had enjoyed her company. They were chattering away like a pair of magpies when Charlotte came upon them in the drawing room.

"Do you realize how late you are?" she chided. "If you have an appointment this evening, you have not got much time to get ready."

Nancy stood very much at ease and looked affectionately at Charlotte. "Oh, it is so good to have you near again. You worry enough for all three of us. You do not know how much I missed it."

Charlotte reached out and gave her hand a squeeze. "Shall you be seeing his lordship tonight, little one?"

Nancy sighed and shook her head. "No, I do not think he is too happy with me. He never came to see me after the performance."

Charlotte and Phoebe gathered round her. "It is the apartment, isn't it?" said Charlotte.

"I daresay."

"Oh, but then we are imposing," exclaimed Charlotte. "I feared that it might be that way."

"Nancy, pet, you ought not to have imposed us upon his lordship," said Phoebe. "It was not at all necessary."

"It was necessary to me," retorted Nancy. "I was

positively perishing from loneliness in this great place. See how much cozier it has become with you here?"

"Yes, but, child, it is his lordship's to dispose of, not yours," Charlotte pointed out.

Nancy shrugged. "I offered to vacate it, but he would not have it."

"I am sure that he never bargained for Phoebe and myself being charges upon him."

"He did not refuse me when I asked him, and I am sure that he never notices the little added expense."

"Little?" exclaimed Charlotte. "You never told us he paid for the board as well. I am sure that Phoebe's charges for food are greater than his own household's— not to say that he receives nothing in return from any of us for this largesse."

"I should be more than happy to arrange to put paid to my bill with his lordship, but I suspect that his interest lies in another direction," said Phoebe, chuckling.

"Oh, Phoebe, it is so bad of you to speak that way," said Nancy.

They had been so busy chatting that they had not heard someone knocking and one of the maids going to the door. Now, suddenly appearing on the threshold of the chamber was Lord Faile, a look of constrained disappointment on his countenance .

"Oh, I say! I do beg your pardon, Nancy. I did not know that you were entertaining."

"Oh, my lord, how nice of you to call. No, I am not entertaining anyone. You know Miss Lequesne and Miss Bell. They have come to stay with me," said Nancy brightly, going over to him and taking him by the hand. To her companions, she said, "You know My Lord Faile, our most gracious benefactor."

Said Phoebe, "My Lord Marquis, I wish there was some way I could make some return to you for this swell accommodation."

Said Charlotte, glaring at Phoebe, "Your lordship, words cannot express our thanks to you for having reunited us with Nancy."

His lordship stood with one hand on his hip while he scratched the back of his head in confusion. "You have already moved in here?"

"Indeed, Tony. What was the point in putting it off? Do you mind?" asked Nancy, studying him.

"Oh, no," he said quickly—too quickly. "It just took me by surprise is all. I, er, had hoped that we, you and I, my dear, could sit and coze for a bit . . . er, in private, you see."

"But of course, Tony. I should be delighted. Charlotte has an engagement this evening, and I am sure that Phoebe can find some place she has got to go. If it would be your pleasure, you and I could have our dinner here. You never have sampled cook's wares, and considering it was you who engaged her, I think you ought."

Lord Faile's features visibly brightened. "Why, yes, I should like that very much."

"Then why do you not depart for a few hours and come back at, say, eight o'clock? That will give us all time to change and for the girls to go about their separate ways."

"Eight o'clock? I shall be here at the striking of the hour."

He raised her hand to his lips and took his leave.

"I suggest that his lordship is not overly pleased with this arrangement," said Phoebe.

Nancy was looking troubled. "He did look taken aback to see you with me. I wonder what it is he wishes to say to me."

Phoebe turned to Charlotte. "It was quite wonderful while it lasted. Do you suppose we can get our garret back, my dear?"

"It does come to that, does it not," responded Charlotte, looking a bit blue.

Said Nancy, trying to be cheerful, "I am sure that we are well enough fixed to do better than a musty old garret this time."

Charlotte shook her head. "Nancy, there is no need for you to leave, too. We can visit each other."

Stubbornly Nancy shook her head. "No! If you must leave, then so must I. It was so nice to be together again, even if it was but for a few days. I pray you will let me come with you."

Said Phoebe, "But of course, if you wish it. We have missed you, too."

Nancy was all smiles as she said, "In that case, Tony can have his old apartment back."

Charlotte remarked, "I think you are being a bit rash, child. It will not help to put my lord marquis out of humor with you."

Nancy shrugged. "I like Tony very much, but he does not possess me in any way and he never shall. I have my career."

Phoebe chuckled and said, "I pray that he will leave *that* much to you. After all, his word at the Opera goes a long way. You'd not have risen so far and so fast had he not been most encouraging and spoken with Coates. You know he must have."

"I assure you that Tony is not at all that sort," retorted Nancy with indignation.

"We shall see what we shall see," said Charlotte. "In the meantime, I have to prepare for the evening, and you had better, too, Phoebe."

"I daresay. I might just as well spend the rest of this day looking for lodgings. I have the strongest feeling that we shall be needing one."

She looked about her at the sumptuous decor of the drawing room and sighed. "I tell you, living here for even these few hours has been the high point of my life. It is a far cry from the best that Billingsgate has to offer, you may rely on it."

Tony ought to have known better. It was a quarter before the hour when he arrived, and the ladies were still some thirty minutes at least from finishing with their toilet. He did not seem to mind, though, and made himself comfortable in the drawing room, with his hostess's permission lighting up a cigar to help him pass the time, listening to the snatches of feminine conversation that came floating out to him from the rear of the apartment.

It was Nancy who came out to him first. She appeared to be a little breathless and apprehensive. "I finished as quickly as I could, Tony. I pray I do not look a sight."

He smiled as he arose to take her by the hand. "Indeed, my pet, you *do* look a sight."

"Oh, Tony!"

"A perfectly enchanting sight. Come sit with me."

They sat down side by side on the divan and Nancy inquired, "What is it that you would say to me?"

"Er . . . we are not as private as I would like. The girls will be leaving soon?"

Nancy glanced at the tall clock standing by the wall and replied, "They are almost ready, but I do not know what is keeping Charlotte's gentleman. Mr. Westley is usually very prompt. But surely, Tony, what you have to say is not all that complicated. I understand that you have no wish to say it before Charlotte and Phoebe to save them embarrassment, but they are not here, and much as I could wish not to have to hear it, I am prepared."

Tony sat up in surprise and looked hard at her. "What do you mean you are prepared? Have I become some sort of an ordeal for you to have to put up with?"

A hurt look came into Nancy's eyes. "My lord, it

must be an ordeal to me when I am to be forced to choose among the people I love most dearly."

"I say!" exclaimed Tony, and he sat staring at her for a few moments. Finally he collected his wits and angrily stated, "I must be the world's greatest fool! Who is he?"

"Who is who?" asked Nancy, bewildered.

"This other dearly beloved. I had no inkling that you were seeing any other chap but me."

"I am not, my lord. Who told you differently?"

"You did, just now."

"I never!"

Her exclamation caused Lord Faile to change his tone. He was solicitous as he replied, "I pray that I am wrong, but I did hear you say that you were having to choose among dear friends. Do I not count as one of them?"

Nancy laughed uncertainly. "But of course, Tony. There is you and there is Charlotte and Phoebe. I thought you knew that."

"Charlotte and Phoebe? Now, how do they come into it? Why in the world must you choose between them and me?"

"Is it not obvious? Must I not have to part with their company if you insist?"

"I am not insisting on anything," he retorted, nettled. "If you have a wish to leave them, do not put it on me."

"But I have to. If they must remove themselves from this apartment, then so must I."

Tony blinked. Very quietly he asked, "And pray, why must they leave this apartment?"

"Because you . . . you . . ." Nancy's voice became very small and faded away. She shook her head and said, "Are you not about to . . . to . . . Tony, what are you wishing to say to me if it is not that?"

"Not what, pet? What the devil are we arguing about? You are the one who brought Charlotte and

Phoebe into this conversation—for what reason, I have yet to discover."

Nancy was beginning to look happier. "Then you were not about to ask me to send them packing?"

"It is certainly a most pleasant prospect, but not unless it is your wish, little one. This is your place to do with as you please; I told you that, I thought."

"Oh, Tony, I am so relieved!" cried Nancy, and threw herself into his arms.

Tony was not at all sure why he should have been so richly rewarded, but he was not one to neglect the harvesting, and sparked by a desire that was ungovernable, he kissed her with a passion.

A mounting ecstasy was kindled between them and the world and all forgot. But it was not meant to last, for at the moment Charlotte and Phoebe came strolling in, both dressed for going out.

"Oh, dear!" Charlotte looked shocked.

Phoebe grinned but said nothing as Tony and Nancy quickly drew apart. While Nancy guiltily put herself in order, Tony laughed in his embarrassment and remarked, "What price privacy!"

Concerned, Charlotte asked, "Nancy, are you all right? I mean to say, it might be wiser if we all of us sat down to dinner together this evening."

Tony's eyes began to mirror his anger at this impertinence, and Phoebe rushed to say, "Heavens, what can be keeping Westley?"

Nancy picked up the cue and said as hastily, "Ah, then you and Charlotte are going out together tonight."

"Yes," said Charlotte, relieved to have her gaff so quickly glossed over. "I am sure that Arthur will not object. He is terribly obliging."

Tony's face was become a picture of exasperation as he inquired, "I take it that your escort ought to have been here by this time."

"Indeed, your lordship, Mr. Westley is never less

than prompt. I do hope that nothing unpleasant has occurred to make him so tardy."

Nancy glanced nervously at Tony, who was staring at the ceiling, and bit her lip. Suddenly she was very unsure of herself. She could not help looking forward to being alone with Tony, but after that kiss, she was not at all sure that she could trust herself and even less sure that she could trust Tony. She said, "Why do you not sit down with us while you wait? I am sure that Arthur will be along shortly."

Tony gave her an unhappy look.

She saw it and a devil took hold of her tongue. She said, as Charlotte and Phoebe seated themselves across the room from the divan, "Tony is delighted that you have come to stay with me."

Tony glared at her, and Phoebe, watching him, burst into forthright laughter. "What a whopper that is," she said.

At that, Tony, too, broke down and began to laugh, reaching out to give Nancy's hand a squeeze.

The maid entered to announce the arrival of Mr. Westley and friend.

Charlotte immediately arose and was on her way to the door when in came Arthur with Sir Richard right behind him. "Arthur, in heaven's name why are you so late? You have managed to embarrass me," she complained.

"Awfully sorry, dear, but you never told me that you had removed yourself from Floral Street. But I say, is not this Faile's place?—er, I beg your pardon, your lordship—I mean to say, Miss Faulconer's lodgings?"

"Oh, how careless of me," said Charlotte. "I never did inform you did I. Yes, this is my new direction. Miss Bell and I have joined Miss Faulconer at her request."

Arthur's face dropped. In great disappointment he said, "But if you had only said that you were unhappy with the Floral Street arrangement, I should have been truly delighted to have assisted you to make another. I mean to say, there is no reason on earth why you should be a burden to my Lord Faile," and he conferred a peculiar look upon the marquis.

Nancy spoke up: "It is none of my lord's doing, Mr. Westley, but if Charlotte should prefer a different ar-range——"

"No, of course I do not! And Arthur, it is most improper in you to have made such a suggestion. I am here at Nancy's express invitation, and whatever is between her and his lordship is neither your business nor mine." By this time her face was crimson as she realized what it was she was implying.

Nancy's face was a picture of despair as she looked to Tony. Lord Faile was absolutely no help, however, for he had gone off into a gale of laughter, in which he was joined only by Phoebe.

Sir Richard was mightily confused and looked to Arthur for an explanation, but the latter was being immolated on the spot by a fiery glance from Charlotte and was at a loss for words.

Finally Tony took pity upon all and sundry and arose to shake hands with Sir Richard. "Ah, Shadworth, I have not seen you about of late. Where have been keeping yourself?"

"I have just returned from Melton, my lord, and apparently in good time, for this, my neighbor in Leicestershire, seems to have developed a knack for falling into the pickle barrel. I pray you will not take offense at his mindless bad taste—but I say! Isn't anyone about to do the proper, or must I do it myself? I am not acquainted with any of these lovely ladies and I am dying to have that lack remedied at once."

Arthur, completely off poise, turned from a hurried conversation with Charlotte to do the honors, but Lord Faile was before him, introducing Nancy to him.

"Ah," said Sir Richard, reaching for his quizzing glass and raising it to his eye to better regard Nancy. Quickly he let it fall to its length of ribbon and bowed. "I am sure that the queen of the Nile must rest content now that you have so brilliantly portrayed her, Miss Faulconer." He turned to Tony. "My lord, your taste is exquisite."

Arthur, who had had his ears burned by Charlotte, put a heavy elbow into his ribs and, startled, Sir Richard turned upon him, quizzing glass to his eye.

Tony took the occasion to introduce Phoebe to Sir Richard, and at once that gentleman forgot about everything else, praising her warmly for her performance in the ballet.

Phoebe had been eyeing him from the moment he had entered the room. She was impressed with his great size, and in that he was little different from Mr. Westley; but that was the only similarity between them. Sir Richard was a swell and could take his stand alongside the likes of Lord Faile. She was sure that she would like him very much indeed. And so, when it turned out that Sir Richard would be both honored and privileged if she would accept him as her escort for the evening, she was both honored and privileged, and more than happy, to accept.

A few minutes later, Nancy and Tony were alone together in the apartment.

CHAPTER SIX

It was a quiet meal they shared in the tiny dining room of the apartment, quiet indeed, as each of them seemed to be wrapped in thought. As it came to an end with brandy for the gentleman and coffee for the lady, the marquis took out his cigar case, selected a cigar, and lit it with one of the candles on the table.

In the act of puffing it to incandescence, suddenly he paused and stared at Nancy. "I beg your pardon, my dear; I never asked your permission." He put the candlestick down upon the table and shifted the cigar from between his fingers to his thumb and first finger. "May I?"

"Whatever is your pleasure, my lord. This is your house."

He frowned and ground the cigar out on a plate before him. "Nancy, there are times when I do not begin to understand you. In fact, I am not sure that I have ever understood you and most especially this very moment."

"Is it so necessary, my lord?"

"You are angry with me."

"Not I, my lord."

"Then what is it that has got you in a mood?"

"I am sure you would find it a bore, my lord."

"I am sure that I would not."

Nancy stared at him from beneath lowered lids. She was not sure how she ought to put into words that which was bothering her. "I fear lest I make you displeased."

"I assure you, little one, nothing you can do would displease me."

"Then I do protest, my lord, at what people are thinking of me."

He stared at the defunct cigar, turned his eyes away from it, and quickly replied, "Why, what do you believe people are thinking of you?"

"They are taking me for your light o' love."

He smiled. "I hardly think so, especially as now you have two doughty chaperones to protect your reputation. By the way, considering the speed with which you brought them here, I am beginning to suspect that you had some such idea in mind. Is it true?"

"No, my lord—not at the time that I first thought of it, at least—but after Arthur Westley implied so much by his offer to Charlotte, it set me to thinking that I had been wise."

"For heaven's sake, Nancy, 'wise'? Damnably inconvenient, I should say. It does not appear that we shall have anything as cozy as this many times in the future with Charlotte and Phoebe about. Is that what you had wished?"

"Perhaps. None of it strikes me as proper, my lord. At least now no one can say that you are keeping me unless they include Phoebe and Charlotte as well."

"That is for certain, and I feel like an idiot about the business."

"You did not have to do it," she pointed out.

"I am not sure of that. What if I had refused your request?"

She cast her eyes down. "I think that I should have had to leave this place, my lord. I could not bear the impropriety of it all."

"That is the second time you have seen fit to bring in the proprieties! What have you, a wench from the ballet, to do with propriety, may I inquire?"

Slowly her eyes came up to meet his. She did not say a word but just stared at him.

There was an edge to his voice as he said, "Nancy, I have a very great affection for you and I could wish that we were more to each other than we are, but I see that you are under some misapprehension with regard to your station in life. You are a girl from the ballet and nothing more. True you are blessed with a talent to make you shine above all the rest, but that still does not add an iota to your prospects beyond the theater. I am sure that you must understand by this time how much *I* can add to your prospects, yet you have not responded to anything that I have suggested. Say something—*anything!* What would you have of me?"

"Nothing, my lord."

"Yet you take whatever I give to you."

"Only because you did insist upon it and I had no wish to make you angry."

He fell back in his chair and looked hard at her. "Only for that reason? I am not in the least flattered. I was under the impression that you did care for me."

"I assure you, my lord, that I do, but you mistake me for something that I am not."

"I am sure I do not. You are Miss Nancy Faulconer, rising young star of the Italian Opera House."

"But I was not bred to it, my lord," said Nancy, a note of desperation in her voice.

"What has that to say to it?"

"My lord, indeed I am flattered that you should make any offer at all to me, but I am not a 'wench from the ballet,' not the light-skirt you imply. Some of the ballerinas are, I daresay—the gossip cannot be denied—but their prospects are not mine and never were. I am merely a milliner's assistant; that is all my upbringing, and I may not enter upon an improper life. Not the sort of thing you offer me."

"What must I do? Offer you marriage? I daresay as a marquise, you would have no objection to returning my affection."

"Tony, I do not like you when you are in this humor."

He took a deep breath. "I cannot say that I am particularly enamored of myself at this moment, either, but you drive me to it."

"Then I fear that we must part."

"Not so fast! You know very well that I cannot allow that."

"I know of no such thing! Tony, what are you saying? You are a *marquis*. You can have any 'wench' from the ballet you wish."

"It appears that that is not true, my pet. There is you, and I sincerely apologize for that uncalled for and most undeserved remark."

Nancy shrugged. "Tony, I am not sure that I can stand more of this. I think I should prefer it if you were to leave."

"Not before we come to an understanding. You do like me, do you not?"

Nancy nodded without looking at him.

"But you will not have me on any terms, correct?"

She remained staring down into her lap.

"For God's sake, girl, since I am not altogether displeasing to you, why not? What precisely are your prospects? I urge you to consider them."

Her head came up and she looked at him with glittering eyes. "They are at least better than poor Fleurette's! What has she to show for all of the years she spent with you? I shall have at least not *that* misery to go through."

"What misery? She has taken up with Arliss and is doing quite well for herself, considering how expensive she is."

"It is not something I could do, Tony, after you were done with me," she said, her voice so filled with defeat it was almost a whisper.

Up went his lordship's eyebrows and his features cleared. "Ah, so we have come to it at last, have we? Very well, I shall make a handsome settlement upon you against the day we part."

She stood up abruptly and declared angrily, "That day will never come, for we shall never begin together! My lord, now it is over time for one of us to leave this place, either you or me!"

He stood up quickly and held out a pleading hand. "Nancy, what in blazes did I say? I thought that that was what you were driving at."

"My lord, earlier this evening you claimed not to be able to understand me. Indeed, that is the truest thing you have ever said, you may rely upon it!"

"Oh, damn and blast!" exclaimed Tony. "All right, I shall leave you now. It is obvious I am bound to keep tripping over my teeth the rest of this night if I stay. But, Nancy, I have not finished with you, and *you* may rely upon *that!* As for this bloody apartment, I am going to buy the damned building and give it to you. That, I do believe, will put an end to all this by-your-leave business. I told you the place was yours and you are the mistress here and I meant it! And now, my lady, good night!"

He stormed from the room, and she heard the front

door slam as she rested her head upon the table and fell to weeping.

Rehearsals began the next day for the new opera, in which there was to be just a bit of dancing. Between the acts, however, the ballet company was to give a special performance featuring their star of the toe dance, Nancy Faulconer.

Unfortunately, the star's ability to apply herself to her art was something impaired. Nancy found that she could not get the conversation of the previous evening out of her mind, and a conviction mounted within her that she had been quite out in her statements. More than the conversation clouded her thinking, though. Tony's face, every expression that had appeared upon his countenance, kept center stage in the theater of her imagination. Every word he had uttered and everything she had said were constantly being reviewed, and needless to say, her work showed it.

As day followed day and no word came from Tony —he did not even make an appearance in the theater, as was his wont—she was more than sure that she had heard the last from him and the conclusion devastated her. She did not wish to see the last of Tony, not ever. That was now eminently clear to her. He was not necessary to her, and she felt lost without a prospect of being with him ever again. It was all so easy to talk about what was supposed to be good and pure, but nothing of the sort counted where Tony was concerned. She knew that now, now that she had lost him. Life was suddenly turned quite miserable for her, and she was sure that she was wrong in rejecting any offer he had a mind to make to her. So what if he tired of her! If she was as fortunate as Fleurette, she might have his company for years, and that was a great deal better than not to have him at all!

So poor was her work at rehearsal that Signor Bouquin called her down for it in front of the company. The shame of the incident brought her mind back to her work and gave birth to the resolution that she must go to Tony and beg his forgiveness, make an attempt to restore their good relations. It was a most desperate resolution, but she could not do anything else, she was sure. She did not know what she would do if Tony was not to be her very good friend anymore.

That evening, as she proceeded to dress for the occasion and to rehearse what she would say to him, the thought came to her that perhaps, discouraged by her adamant refusal, he had gone to seek solace in some other female's arms. The idea quite destroyed her, and she was powerless to go on with her toilet.

Charlotte and Phoebe had assumed that she was going out with Tony, but, as they too had engagements this night, the one with Westley, the other with Shadworth, and were quite busy themselves preparing, they did not notice Nancy's preoccupation until it was almost time for their gentlemen to come for them. They were just beginning to remonstrate with her for being so far behind in her dressing when they were all interrupted by a maid coming in to them with a packet for Nancy.

Eagerly Nancy reached for it and tore it open. It contained a legal-looking document and a note. Holding the document in one hand, she quickly scanned the note and then, falling to weeping, cast the papers from her.

Both Charlotte and Phoebe were very much concerned to know what was wrong, but Nancy refused to respond, her tears flowing and her sobs racking her slight frame.

Charlotte, close to her wit's end, decided that, privacy or no, she had better read what was written in the papers Nancy had cast down in her despair. Who had sent them might provide a clue. She knelt and gathered them up, giving a batch to Phoebe while she kept what appeared to be an accompanying note. Immediately she saw that it was from the marquis of Faile, but it did not appear that he had written anything to evince such sorrow as Nancy was displaying.

Phoebe took one look at the papers in her hand and declared, "This is legal stuff! I am not an attorney, Charlotte. Here, you take it. What has yours got to say?"

"It is from the marquis—our landlord? I say, precisely what is the marquis to us? But he has given the lease to Nancy! He is *nothing* to us any longer."

"Oh, I should not have done it!" cried Nancy, mopping at her eyes. She reached for the note and waved it about, saying, "Tony is displeased with me; that is why he has done this thing. You see, it gives him the excuse for never having to come here again."

Charlotte said, "I am blessed if I understand how you come to draw that conclusion. His lordship has made a valuable gift to you. London leases, especially in this district, are very expensive. Had he actually promised to buy this house for you?"

Nancy nodded. "But not because he meant it as a gift. He was wroth with me for reminding him that he it was who could do as he pleased here, as it was his place. And now you see what he has gone and done, don't you?"

Charlotte took the letter from her and reread it. She shrugged her shoulders and said, "I still do not see the need for tears, my dear. He says he tried to buy the place but a great fortune was being asked for it. I can believe that. London real estate is far and away out of sight when it comes to purchasing it. You have got to be as wealthy as Lord Faile to be able to afford even the lease in this district. I am sure he did his best, and you should be grateful."

"Oh, you do not understand! It is his way of giving me a setdown because I would not——" She caught her lip between her teeth as she blushed. She could not go on.

Charlotte laughed and turned to Phoebe. "And you call *me* missish? Have you ever heard of such a tempest in a teapot as is this? Nancy, I cannot believe that of Lord Faile. He is not that sort of chap; I am sure of it."

"If that is so, pray inform me as to what I am going to do with this lease. I can never afford it. Not all three of us paying into it every copper we earn can afford it. I shall have to sell it and we shall have to move. In fact, if it should prove that the rent is due, we shall be hard put to hold ourselves together long enough to find another buyer for the place, or whatever you call them."

"Good heavens, I never thought of that!" exclaimed Charlotte, turning pale. "Whatever are we going to do?"

"I suggest that we wait until my Lord Faile comes round to inform us," put in Phoebe. "There is something here that is all terribly confusing. I should have been willing to bet a year's wages that his lordship would never do the least thing to hurt the little one for the simple reason that he is in love with her."

"Oh, that is perfect nonsense!" said Nancy heatedly. "His lordship does not know the meaning of the word! It is all some sort of monstrous game to him. Don't you see, if he cannot buy what he desires, he casts it aside and goes on to something that is within his reach. Besides, what business does a marquis have falling in love with a ballet girl? Phoebe, you are not being very bright."

"I am sure that that has nothing to do with it. I have the strongest premonition that Mr. Westley would ask me to marry him if I gave him the smallest bit of encouragement, which I am not about to—not yet, at any rate," remarked Charlotte.

"Oh, but that is different," said Nancy. "Charlotte, being a ballet dancer is not the greatest thing in your life as it is in mine. You are of the gentry and are bound to find yourself a gentleman. I am a ballet dancer and nothing more, with no prospect of ever rising higher than the stage. Considering my beginnings, that is very great distance for one such as I," pointed out Nancy.

Phoebe nodded and added, "True, Charlotte, it is different for us than it is for you. I am not any fool to believe that the light in Sir Richard's eyes for me is anything honorable. He is not your Mr. Westley in any respect. Ah, I wish I could share your feelings and be able to say that if Mr. Westley asked *me,* I should not be impressed, but I should and there it is. I have had my fill of Sir Richards and Lord Failes. I am not so sure that I shall not end my days back in Billingsgate if they are all the sort of gentlemen I can expect to meet."

"Why, Phoebe, I thought that you had a very good time with Sir Richard! I am positive that he did, too. Arthur has said as much to me."

"Oh, I pray you will not misunderstand me. I am sure that Sir Richard is a most attractive gentleman. It is just that he is like all the rest. He eyes me as though he were a great fox and I a plump prize hen. I mean to say, cannot men think of anything else?"

Charlotte's eyes opened wide. "Phoebe, is that you speaking—truly?"

Phoebe laughed. "Aye, I am just talking. I know they will never change and we must make the best of it, which is precisely what I intend to do."

"Really!" interposed Nancy. "What a conversation to be having at a time like this! What are we going to do for lodgings, I ask you?"

"Truly, child, it is early days to worry about that. Why do you not go out with us—one of us—and take your mind off it?"

"Thank you but no. I . . . I think I ought to wait a bit. It is just possible that his lordship will decide to come round. After all, we did have an appointment for this evening and he has not called it off."

"A very wise suggestion," said Charlotte. "If he should happen by, you can ask him outright precisely what this gesture of his means."

"Yes," agreed Nancy, while in her mind she was thinking that it would be something if Tony even just came to call.

The ladies then proceeded to prepare themselves for their evening's engagements.

CHAPTER SEVEN

Nancy was alone in the apartment. She was seated in the drawing room, fully dressed in a creation she had never worn before, one she felt particularly suited her small figure and petite face.

The gown, high-waisted, was of poppy-colored silk with a low neckline, made modest by a tucker of *crêpe lisse* folded *à la Farinet* and confined in front and at the shoulders by tiny pearl loops. The skirt was something fuller than the old Empire cut and was ornamented at the bottom with a rouleau of darker hue to match the girdle. Two flounces trimmed the hem. The sleeves were short and full, just coming over the shoulder to the arm.

Her head was adorned with a plaited satin band, set well back from her forehead so that it did not overshadow her countenance, especially as it carried plumes of the bird of paradise laid along it. Her hair was heaped up from behind and carefully combed and parted before. White gloves of kid extending above the elbow completed her attire, and beside her on the divan cushion was a Chinese fan.

She had seen the design in *Ackermann's Repository,* the style periodical. The illustration was of Mackenzie tartan, but she had had it made up in a solid color with some slight modification. Charlotte had approved.

In her hand was the lease, rolled up, which she batted into her palm every now and again as she sat and thought about it. She tried to recall the precise circumstances in which Tony had made a vow to give her the place, the temper he had been in, what he had said, and what *she* had said to have brought it on. She wished to think that Charlotte was correct in her surmise and that the lease was the best that he could do in that direction; but a lease called for rent to be paid, and although she had not the faintest idea of what it would amount to, she was sure it would be far more than she could afford.

On the other hand, if Tony was withdrawing his attention from her, then this must be quite a slap in her face. The sale of the lease would be in a sense a sort of settlement—which she had never wanted—and she would be out, along with Charlotte and Phoebe, to find a place of less pretentiousness . . . and to suffer the slings of Madame Fleurette's gloating. Nothing she could say to Fleurette—or to anyone else, for that matter—would convince her that she was not nor had ever been anything to Tony but a friend. Invalid though it might be, there would be a strong sense of disgrace and defeat that must attend her surrendering the apartment. But that would be like nothing compared to the sense of loss accompanying Tony's withdrawal of his protection and, perhaps even his notice. That would be the cruelest cut of all.

Oh, if only he would come and not let it rest like that! Whatever her future had in store for her as a brilliant ballerina, it would be less than nothing if Tony were not a part of it. It was something that she had always suspected but never dwelt upon. She had not thought that anything would intervene. She was not Tony's mistress so that, even if he had wed his marquise, when he came to that decision, his friendly interest in her would continue.

But it was beginning to appear that life could never be so simple. Tony wanted her and that, of course, was most flattering, but it did not point to anything for herself. All she could look forward to beyond the pleasure of his company for a month or a year was to be discarded even as he had set Fleurette aside in *her* favor. Then again, what more could she expect? She was not Charlotte, with a fine family background, to be able to demand a more respectable dealing from a gentleman. Rise as high as she might in her profession, her lack of gentle blood must forever stand in the way of so exalted a marriage. It was not unheard of for a high gentleman to take a commoner to wife, but it was far and away a most unlikely eventuality, and assuredly no milliner's assistant had ever risen so high.

Perhaps, for whatever happiness she desired, she must accept Tony on any terms he deigned to offer her. While their relationship lasted, she could make believe that it would go on forever and yet, knowing how it must end, not be slain when she was displaced. She sighed a sigh of resignation. It was as much as she could hope for, if only she was not too late. If Tony would but call as he had engaged to do, there might still be time to start over with him—on his terms.

But where was Tony? It was getting on and there was not the slightest indication of his coming, not even a message. It was not like him; he was more considerate than that. Ah, but then it could be that no news was good news at this turn. Perhaps he was coming, she

tried to tell herself, and that is why she had not heard
from him. He was late, that was all.

She looked at the clock in the corner. It was after
nine, and he had made the appointment for half-past
eight. The girls and their escorts had departed a half-
hour ago. She almost wished that she had gone with
them. The clock was the poorest company.

When the clock struck the half-hour, Nancy was softly sobbing, now quite convinced that Tony was through
with her and there was no point in her waiting for him
any longer. She might as well retire to her room, not to
sleep, heaven knows—she could never sleep now—but
to plan on disposing of the lease and finding new quarters.

With the realization that tomorrow would be just another day to live through, she stood up and dabbed at
her eyes with her handkerchief. There would be no
thrill in the ballet for her any longer—or in anything
else, as far as that went.

She stood up straight and listened, her whole body
tense. Was that a knock on the apartment door?

Yes, it was!

It had to be Tony; it *must* be Tony, she thought, as
she raced out of the room toward the front door. She
waved away the maid, who was on her way to answer
it, and, without pausing to put herself in order, threw
the door wide open.

It *was* Tony!

"Tony! Tony!" she cried, and threw herself into his
arms, the tears streaming down her cheeks.

Tony had been standing at the door, a smile of anti-
cipation on his face. It quickly changed to one of dumb-
founded astonishment as the little bundle in his arms
continued to sob as though her heart were breaking.

He eased Nancy and himself inside and closed the
door behind them. "I *say*," he exclaimed, "what's

wrong?" He made no attempt to free himself of her but held her to him as, with his free hand under her chin, he gently raised her face to his.

He would have said more, but the look in her pretty little face quite took his breath away and he leaned down and kissed her warmly. It did nothing to help him regain his breath, but it did stop Nancy's weeping. In fact, the world was at a standstill for those breathless moments.

"Now, what the devil is this all about? One would have thought I had just returned from the dead. Great heavens, girl, do you miss me that much? I was only a few minutes late. My cariage broke down in the middle of Oxford Street and I had to walk home and make other arrangements."

He chuckled. "It is rather amusing when you come to think of it. In these modern times we do not think of walking if we can ride, even if we have to walk to manage it. I am so sorry, my pet. If I had known that you were so worried for me, I'd have come right on in a cab and let the blasted trap lay."

They were standing by the divan and he took her into his arms. "I am rather touched," he said and kissed her again. Then he handed her down to the seat and stood before her. "Where would you like to go tonight?" he asked.

Nancy was still having a time of it untangling the welter of confusion that was her mind. There was absolutely nothing in Tony's attitude to lend credence to her suspicions regarding the lease. He could not have intended anything to her discomfit. He could never have kissed her so . . . so thoroughly, she was sure.

Still holding his hand, she looked up at him and said, "Tony, it was more than that. I did not think that you were coming. The . . . the lease . . . it was as though you were saying good-by to me, for surely you know I could never manage to keep it up and must either sell it or return it to you. After our last conversation, I thought that it was all over between us and I liked to die."

Tony sat down beside her and looked directly into her eyes. There was a slight frown on his brow as he gave her hand a little shake and said, "Now, would not that have been a rather odd sort of present to one I hold very dear? Nothing has changed on that score, little one, nothing at all. I gave you the lease so that you would be assured that you are the mistress of this place and I am not the master, as you seem to believe. Never worry about the upkeep; it is still in my province. I admit, had it been possible to buy the place, it would have made my intent more clear, but the owners would sooner sell their birthright. They would not even put a price upon it."

Then he smiled broadly. "But, if the result of the misunderstanding is productive of such sweet confusion, I say let misunderstanding reign forever between us." With that, he enfolded her in his arms once more and all conversation ceased.

Again there was a shortage of breath, and it took a while for the both of them to regain a semblance of composure.

It was Nancy who spoke first. What she had to say was not easy for her. Tony was not in any mood for conversation, however, and she was forced to put her hand against his chest. He did not press himself forward, but neither did he retreat, and they sat like that for a bit while she spoke:

"Tony, I have something to say to you." She paused to gaze at him to gauge his mood.

He was still a little out of breath as he said, "Is it so all-fired important that you must needs speak of it now, this very moment, this instant?"

"Y-yes, Tony, it is. I would have you know that I have changed my mind."

He smiled. "Oh, is that all? As it is the prerogative of your gender, I do not see that further discussion is at all necessary. These past few minutes rather impressed me with the fact." He resettled himself in his seat and clasped his hand over hers where it rested on his breast. "Now, then, I do not think that either of us has an overwhelming desire to go out tonight, have we?"

"Whatever you wish, my lord," replied Nancy in a submissive tone.

At once Tony's eyes lit up and he started to move closer. "I say, but this is more like it. It was the lease that did the trick, wasn't it," he said, very well pleased with himself.

Nancy did not remove her hand but, still gazing into his eyes, shook her head.

"It was not?" asked Tony, stopping still and cocking his head. "I was sure it must have been. What was it, then?"

Nancy dropped her hand into her lap and replied, "Oh, the lease had something to do with it, my lord. I had thought it was a signal of your displeasure and I should not be seeing you again. I . . . I would not have liked that."

Tony's eyebrows shot up in disbelief. "It was just the pleasure of my company, you mean to say? *That* is what has brought about this great change in you?"

"Yes, my lord."

Tony appeared to be somewhat discomposed by her affirmation. He tried again: "My dear, this little gesture of my mine is worth something in the neighborhood of the value of a handsome coach, and you mean to say that that fact had nothing to do with the business?"

"No, Tony. What do I know of carriages or, for that matter, of leases? It was you, my lord. I feared to lose you."

"But you never had me!"

"I had your interest and your company, my lord," said Nancy, biting her lip. She could not fathom Tony's strange behavior. This was not a time for debate.

"Indeed, Miss Faulconer, I should be very flattered if I believed you."

"Good heavens, Tony, what is so strange in it? I am in love with you. Is that so incredible?"

"Oh, for God's sake!" exploded Tony, leaping up from the couch as though suddenly it was too uncomfortable to bear. He started to walk about the room with his hands folded behind him and came to a stop before her. "You are saying this just to put me at a disadvantage, aren't you?" he challenged her.

"My lord, I do not understand you. Is it not what you wished all this while?"

"Of course not! Why, this takes all the sport out of it. You make me feel as though I am taking advantage of you. How can we treat together if you are in love with me? Oh, what a foul mess this is!"

Nancy was devastated. She could not know how things would go on with them after she came to her declaration, but she never suspected that Tony would be anything less than delighted with the prospect, and here he was behaving as though she had done something quite awful.

It was obvious that he did not return her affection, and she was at a loss to understand what it was he wished of her, but not for more than a moment's thought, for the conclusion was self-evident. To Tony, she was not a person at all but merely a replacement for Fleurette—and his opinion of that lady was hardly flattering. In truth, because she was in love with him, she must succeed to Fleurette's place in his regard, to be but a toy for his every whim and never anything more until he tired of her. Then it would be over and she would not even have the dream of a make-believe romance. It was too, too sad, and the tears began to stream down her cheeks.

"There! You see what comes of this childish nonsense? Tears! How am I expected to deal with that? I mean, what fun is it to have to treat with a watery-eyed female? My dear, you are not at your best with the waterworks overflowing."

Which hardly went very far to stem the flood.

"Oh, damn and blast!" exclaimed Tony. "Nancy, you are embarrassing me!"

"My lord, you are hurting me," she replied softly, as though it were too painful to raise her voice.

Tony stood stricken. His face paled and he quickly sat down beside her, taking her hands in his. "Dearest little one, I never intended that. Please, I beg you to believe me. It is just that I am not prepared for this situation. I mean to say, how can we go on together now? If you are in love with me, then I must be on my honor not to take advantage of you, and how in heaven's name am I to know that? It is monstrously unfair of you to fall in love with me. It was so different with Fleurette. We each of us knew the tally and there was nothing to get in the way. I mean to say that . . . well, we were considerate of each other, of course, but . . . but . . ." He stopped, at a loss to put his meaning into words.

"There was no tenderness between you," put in Nancy helpfully.

"Precisely! I am so pleased you understand."

Nancy threw herself down upon the divan and began to sob.

For a moment Tony had a most helpless expression on his face; then he dropped to his knees beside her and gathered her into his arms, holding her close to him while she wept on. There was more than solicitude in him as he brushed her brow with his lips and whispered, "Sweet, I detest having to wear watered silk. This coat you are in the process of ruining cost a pretty penny. Come, dry your eyes and we shall talk some more. Nothing is so bad as you think."

She raised her head and said, all dewy-eyed, "Tony, you will never leave me, will you?"

"That must follow, mustn't it," he said with a sigh of resignation. "This is what comes of falling in love. Well, the die is cast and I have only myself to blame. I ought to have been forewarned. A milliner's assistant brought up on romantic novels, no doubt. You have read novels, I venture to guess?"

Nancy nodded and smiled shyly.

"I thought as much. Well, my pet, I cannot promise never to leave you, but I do not see that as any reason why we cannot continue on as we have for a bit. I seem to have lost my bearings or I know I should never agree to it, but there it is," he said briskly as he got to his feet.

"Come, let us get out of this. I have a deal of thinking to do and I know that I cannot do it here. Let us go out for the evening. I say! Over at the Coburg they are exhibiting what they claim is a genuine Italian ballet troupe. I am sure that must take your mind off things for a bit; mine too. Let us go and see, and another time we shall sit down together and talk. I have the strongest presentiment that all that will be said between us has not been said, if that makes any sense to you. Egad! For the moment, I am at a loss as to what I shall do with you, but for now, I should much rather have you with me than anyone else."

Nancy had no idea of all that she was wishing, but this seemed to her a pleasant enough way to begin. She came up off the divan into his arms, and he kissed her with a wildness that both soothed and stirred her at the same time.

CHAPTER EIGHT

For a time things appeared to have settled down. Nancy was seeing Lord Faile, Charlotte was continuing to go out with Mr. Westley, and Phoebe seemed quite content to be entertained by Sir Richard.

Their work at the Opera went on apace, and a month went by with the ladies content with their lot, to all appearances; but appearances were misleading. Nancy and Tony were actually dealing at arm's length with each other. It was as though for them to get too close was to ignite a conflagration that neither one of them knew how to deal with. Nancy would have welcomed it but for the fact that it promised naught but the ecstasy of the moment, while Tony was still trying to find a way to deal with a girl who loved him and for whom he had a depth of affection he dared not explore.

Charlotte was growing more and more fatigued with Arthur's gentle manner towards her, especially as it was accompanied by a never-ending bath of encomiums upon the beauties and attractions of the rural economy.

Of them all, only Phoebe was in the highest state of satisfaction with her new acquaintance. He was a "regu-

lar sort of chap," ready for all sorts of fun, and there
was a roughness to his manner that put her in mind of
some of the Billingsgate swains with whom she had
felt a deal more comfortable than most of the high-
nosed gentlemen she had gone out with since coming
with the Opera.

As for Westley and Shadworth, who roomed together
in the latter's lodgings, things were not going as
smoothly as could have been wished. Sir Richard took
great exception to Arthur's way with Charlotte and did
not hesitate to express himself upon that score:

"You are a bloody, perishing fool, Westley! You do
not know the first thing about the Sex and yet you
proceed along, putting yourself in jeopardy every time
you go out with her."

"The devil you say! Why do you not mind your own
business? I know as much as I need to know, and, I
am thinking it is a deal more useful to me than all of
your bloody nonsense. I am attending upon a *lady*.
What, may I ask, is *your* fair one's claims to gentility?"

"You idiot! It is not wedlock that is my first consideration with the girl! I am out to have a good time, and
she is jolly and accommodating and a beauty to boot.
What more can a man ask?"

"Bah! We are speaking at cross-purposes. You do
what you will and leave me to attend to my own concerns. Miss Bell is not my idea of a proper companion
for a gentleman."

Sir Richard grinned. "Aye, I am glad we agree on
one point. There is a definite air of impropriety about
her that I find most charming. She is a deal more alive
than that cold fish of *yours*."

"I ought to tap your claret for that remark," said
Arthur, balling up his great fists but never making a
move to rise from his chair.

"You are welcome to try. I should not mind having

another go at you, Westley. I think it would be quite a mill after our friendly set-to at Gentleman Jackson's. Actually, I resent your having put off the gloves after you knocked me down. I do not think you could do it again."

"I imagine I caught you by surprise, Richard. I know nothing of the sort of fisticuffs you practice here in London."

"So long as you admit I am the better man."

Arthur chuckled. "Pugilistically speaking, perhaps; but if you would care to try me in a few wrestling holds, I think that you would be in for more devastating surprises than you received at Jackson's Academy."

"Perhaps, but it still does not make any sense the way you go about mooning over this Miss Lequesne of yours?"

"I pray you will leave the lady out of this discussion."

"How can I when it is she and yourself we are discussing?"

"*I* am not discussing anything with you on that score."

"It so happens that that is precisely what I am discussing with you. I hate like the dickens to see a good friend make an ass of himself over a . . . a——"

"Don't say it!" warned Arthur, placing his hands on the side of his chair, ready to launch himself at his friend.

Sir Richard raised a hand and said with a laugh, "All right, I shall not say it. You appear to know what I mean and that is enough."

"What the devil is on your liver anyway? What, actually, do you have against Miss Lequesne? She is a lady in every respect but her blasted profession, and marriage to me must take her out of it. I assure you she could take her place in Leicestershire society and no one would blink an eye."

"You keep straying from the point I would make, my

friend. I have nothing against Miss Lequesne. Surely she is a lady—she has the manner and the sentiment—but whoever heard of anyone but a lump going to the theater to seek out a wife?"

"It is quite possible that many have missed a good bet by not doing so."

"Look you, lad, the whole idea of it was for you to get a bit of bronzing. Burn me if you aren't taking your fences much too fast. A chap looks for a number of things in the lady he would honor by making her his wife. There is the matter of a dowry, and I take it that you can manage any settlements upon her with ease. But then there is the matter of family, and she hasn't any! I mean to say, no doubt she comes of fine stock, but where is it? She is the last of her line, I understand, and that does not speak well for the enduring qualities of her blood."

"My dear Sir Richard, when you come to speak of breeding matters, don't! I am a farmer, an expert in such things, and I tell you you speak absolute balderdash. In any case, I would not wed Charlotte for breeding me a litter. The thought is revolting."

"The thought of *marriage* is revolting."

"Damn you, it is not you who wish to wed; it is I!"

"Nevertheless, the whole idea of it, that you, who have yet to sow your oats, should submit yourself to this . . . this state before you know what is what in the world is . . . is monstrous!"

"My dear Richard, you rave on with all the sense of the King of Bedlam. To me, the holy state of matrimony is most devoutly to be desired. I picture myself with my good wife beside me, surveying with pride what I have wrought in my fields——"

Sir Richard burst into laughter. "Your good wife, the ballet dancer? A farmer's wife? I admire the strength of your imagination but never its clear-sightedness."

"Oh, what is the use of talking to you! Someday it

will come to you and you will know what I mean. For now, it is a waste of breath to even hint at it."

"Again I agree with you, my chum. Indeed it is a waste of breath. I think it would be far wiser if we put your Edenish ideas to the test. You declare that a ballet dancer can make a wife to a farming gentleman, and I declare that you are wrong. What is more, I am willing to put up a purseful of bills that I am right and you are wrong. Do you accept the wager?"

"I would and without the least hesitation except that I do not see any way in which the wager could be resolved."

"How much are we speaking of?"

"It is your bet; you set the stakes."

"A monkey."

Arthur blinked and looked uncomprehendingly at Sir Richard. "A monkey?"

"Five hundred pounds, you nit! Don't you know anything?"

"I say! I could fill my pens with sheep for such a sum!"

"It is your bed we speak of, not your pens."

Arthur's cheeks took on a ruddy hue. "Your way with words, old thing, leaves something to be desired."

"Don't be missish. Do we have a wager?"

"Very well, five hundred pounds it is."

Sir Richard rose from his chair with a grin and offered his hand to Arthur. He got up and they shook on it.

"Now, pray tell me, how are we to go about making the determination?"

Sir Richard rubbed his hands together. "It is quite simple, my boy. All we have got to do is this. . . ."

Arranging the wager, as it turned out, proved to be a deal easier than carrying out its conditions. It seemed that the essential requirement called for getting Charlotte away from the City, and, as both gentlemen intended to be present at the trial, it was necessary that Phoebe come along, too, for Sir Richard wanted his own company.

When Sir Richard approached Phoebe with the idea of an outing into the country, she was delighted and left the day and the time pretty much up to him, which, of course, he deemed only natural. Arthur Westley, on the other hand, ran right into a problem with Charlotte on the same question. Oh, yes, she would be quite pleased to join him on such a jaunt, but she was not sure when she would be free for a sufficient time.

Arthur was very crestfallen when he went to confer with his host on her response. Sir Richard and he were in the farmer's lodgings. It was late morning and they had both just arisen, each having spent the previous evening with his current interest. Coffee and sweet buns had been set out by Tompkins, Sir Richard's man, and the two friends were sitting down to break their fast.

Sir Richard was in high spirits and was rubbing his hands together as he remarked, "Cat got your tongue, old chap? You've been awfully quiet. Not feeling ill, I pray?"

Arthur, having just placed a gob of butter on his hot bun, did not bother to spread it about but just dumbly watched it melt down into a golden murky pool.

"I say, Westley, are you there? In a bit of a fog, aren't you?"

"Huh? Oh, Shadworth, are you addressing me?"

Sir Richard made a business of looking about the room before he replied, "Stab me if there is anyone else about for me to address, old man! What is eating at you? I say, did you make a night of it? Then you are more blessed than I am. This Phoebe, now, she is full of promises, but for one reason and another, it is all I seem to be able to get out of the girl. Promises!"

"That is something more than I have ever got," said

Arthur bitterly. "Did you ask Miss Bell to go out to the country with you?"

"Aye, I did and got another promise. Oh well, I pray that this one she will meet."

"*I* could not get that much."

Sir Richard's eyebrows shot up. "You mean to say Miss Lequesne turned you down flat? This is the female for whom you entertain such glorious prospects?"

"Actually, she did not turn me down outright. In fact, I am not sure that she turned me down at all. I . . . I am not sure *what* she did."

Sir Richard took a large bite out of his bun and washed it down with a sip of hot coffee, then he shook his head forebodingly. "My dear friend, it begins to appear to me as though you have lost the wager before we are ever begun."

"Not quite. I tell you that it is not as if she said no flatly. What she did say was that she would be happy to join us but could not say precisely when."

"Did she give you any reason?"

"Yes, and that is the puzzle in the matter."

"What did she say?"

"She did not know when she could find the time to spare during the week. It would have to be on a Sunday, when the theater is closed."

"Nonsense!" replied Sir Richard. "Phoebe said no such thing to me! Well, there you have it, old man; she turned you down. You might as well fork over and forget her."

"You are most encouraging," snapped Arthur irately.

"You do not have to bite my head off. I am merely presenting you with the fact of the matter. Miss Lequesne has other things to do with her time that take precedence over you. I hardly think it matters a damn bit if she prove herself suitable to being a farmer's wife, under the circumstance."

"Your logic is irrefutable, I will admit, but I am not

in any hurry to dismiss Miss Lequesne from my life. I mean to say, she was perfectly warm and friendly when she said it, you see. I say, do you think she can possibly be so destitute that she *must* labor for her subsistence?"

"A lady? Never!"

Arthur snarled, "I wish you would not be so damned positive. It *is* possible, you know. I mean, there are gentlewomen engaged as companions and governesses. She was one herself, you know."

"Ah, you did say that she had been a governess. Did you think to check her references?"

"Are you out of your skull, Shadworth? Am I to ask references from the woman for whom I entertain a mountain of affection?"

"No, I do not suppose you could do that, but, I say, is it not a peculiar way to go? For a female to take charge of a chap's children, she has got to have references, but to take charge of the chap himself—if you see what I mean."

"Blast you, Shadworth, you have not a romantic bone in your body!" charged Arthur.

Sir Richard beamed broadly. "Yes, I am blessed above all others in regard to that nonsense."

"Bah!"

"Just say if we have done with the wager."

"We have not!"

"Then, pray tell, how does it come about that Miss Bell can go with us any time and Miss Lequesne can not?"

"That is just an added complication."

"My word, but it is not 'just'!"

"Don't nag at me! I have got to think."

"It is perfectly clear to me."

"Then explain it to me."

"She has no desire for your company."

"Tripe! I am seeing her tonight and I did not have to beg."

"Puts an entirely different light upon the business, don't you know."

Arthur pushed aside the bun, on which the butter had recongealed, drew up the saucer, on which rested his cup, and took a sip. "Damn!" he exploded. "It is icy cold!"

"I'll have Tompkins get you another."

"No, thank you. I am not in a mood for any."

"You do not seem to be in a mood for anything."

"How would you feel if you had such a puzzle thrust upon you?"

"I should admit defeat like a brave fellow and pay up."

"Bah!"

"Then what in heaven's name are you about to do?"

"I shall have to trust to her word, shan't I? We shall appoint this Sunday for the outing."

"And if she should find some other outrageous excuse for putting it off, what then?"

"In that case, like the brave fellow I am, I shall admit defeat and pay up."

Sir Richard sat back in his chair with a shrug. "Oh, well, the rhino will spend just as well after a week of waiting for it, I suppose."

If twelve months ago Charlotte had been invited by a gentleman to dine out with him, she would have been highly insulted, for then she had been a governess but yet a lady. Although her pretensions to gentility were slight, they were genuine.

In retrospect, however, she had not been treated like a lady by her former employers—that is, the sires of her charges invariably made approaches to her that resulted in her discharge or her yielding of her post. One day she discovered that she had had quite enough of being a governess, as her beauty made of that position a thing of peril. Upon seeing a notice in the newspapers calling for recruits to the ballet company of the Italian Opera House, she had given over her job without the courtesy of giving notice and become a member of the corps.

In so doing, she had not, in her opinion, surrendered her privileges. She maintained herself in her own opinion and the regard of her friends and colleagues, a lady—at least as far as circumstances would permit. After a time with the Opera, she had come to the realization that she was never going to meet anyone of interest if she continued unyielding on *every* count, and little by little had grown to compromise with the demands of her breeding. Perhaps the greatest concession she had made to date was allowing Mr. Westley, an unexceptional gentleman, to take her out to dine. It had been difficult to be at ease at first, but she'd relied upon her own good judgment and taste to see that she did not overstep the bounds beyond repair to her reputation.

Since she'd joined the ballet, only Mr. Westley had secured any part of her favor, and she had been going out with him on a fairly regular basis for many months. She understood that he might be nursing a tendre for her, but she did nothing to encourage him, being quite content to have found a gentleman to treat her as a lady ought to be treated. She was well aware of the ill-repute with which women of the theater, most especially the unknowns like herself, were regarded.

Mr. Westley seemed to sense something of her feelings, for he managed to find places that would provide them with some privacy. The inns and hotels they dined at were of a better class and so were ever able to provide a private room for them where they could talk freely. Actually, it was the only way that could be allowed. Not for anything would she have accepted an invitation from Mr. Westley to dine at his quarters, not that he was free to invite her, since his lodgings were not his own but those of his host, Sir Richard Shadworth. And, of course, it was unthinkable that she would suggest her own lodgings, which were truly not her own but those of the brilliant young dancing star, and her dear friend, Nancy Faulconer.

By tonight, Charlotte was quite inured to dining out with a gentleman, and although she could have wished that it was her very own husband and her very own menage, still an evening out with Mr. Westley was to be preferred to the usual entertainments that ballet girls managed to find for themselves.

Arthur stared at Charlotte across the white table-cloth. He was partaking of a brandy while she sipped a cordial. It was one of the advantages of dining in private that one could order whatever one wished without having to make excuses. If a lady desired something a bit stronger than coffee or tea or ratafia, she was perfectly free to do so.

Charlotte looked at Arthur and smiled, a question in her eyes.

He looked embarrassed and began to fiddle with a spoon.

"Is there something the matter, Arthur?"

"As long as you have brought the subject up, I fear that there is . . . a bit."

"It concerns me?"

"As long as you mention it, it does . . . a bit."

"Dear me, is this to be some sort of guessing game? Why do you not speak what is on your mind?"

He made a small face and said, "It is no reflection upon you, my dear—not in any way at all, you must understand."

"All right, but if it is of such little consequence, I do not see that there is anything to be made of it."

"Well, there is not, and yet perhaps there is something . . ."

"Yes?"

He had not been looking at her and now he did, rather too brightly. "Yes?" he asked.

Charlotte fell back in her chair, shaking her head in doubt, a small puzzled smile upon her lips. "Truly, Arthur, I do not know what to make of this. Have you something to say or do you not? I suspect that whatever it is, it is not particularly flattering or you would have got it out by this time."

"Ah . . . er . . . as long as you bring up the point, perhaps I ought to explain."

"Yes, I think that would be an excellent idea, or we shall be at this conversation forever and neither one much the wiser for it."

"Yes, precisely."

There was a pause and Charlotte waited. She did not think that any sort of offer was forthcoming, not with such a beginning, or she would have brought the conversation to a close right away. She did not wish to have to refuse Arthur, but she knew she would and their meetings must then come to an end. "Arthur, if you have changed your mind and prefer not to speak, it is perfectly all right with me. After all, I did not bring it up; you did."

"Bring what up, my dear?" he asked, looking blank.

"I think we ought to change the topic, although what it was we were speaking of, I have not the faintest idea."

"Precisely." Then: "Why is it that you cannot go out with me to the country before Sunday and Miss Bell can?" he blurted out with a rush.

"Well, I do declare! If it is so important that you go out to the country and have a wish to take Phoebe with you, please feel free, Mr. Westley. Who am I to say with whom you may or may not go out," said Charlotte, quite provoked.

"Oh, my dear, I do beg your pardon. That was not what I meant at all."

"It seemed perfectly clear to me, Mr. Westley. If you prefer Miss Bell's company to my own, I assure you I have not the least objection."

"You still do not understand," he said plaintively. "I have no wish to go out with Miss Bell."

"Then why are you?"

"But I am not."

"But you just said——"

"Oh, to blazes with what I just said! I spoke like a fool. What I meant to say was that I was troubled over the fact that Miss Bell accepted Sir Richard's invitation to the country without reservation, whereas you have made an excuse to postpone it till Sunday. I mean to say, if you *have* to earn your living, I am sure that she does even more so, for it is obvious to me she is not of the gentry. So I naturally presumed that if she could leave the Opera at any time, certainly you could, too."

Charlotte began to chuckle. "A-and th-this is what has so troubled you?"

"I say, I do hope I am not making an ass of myself."

"It is a little late, my dear sir, for you have already managed it."

Arthur's cheeks turned pink. "I humbly beg your pardon," he murmured. "It was never my inten-tion——"

"Oh, Arthur, I assure you I have every wish for the outing, but it happens that I do have to work, and it hardly makes any difference whether or not Phoebe appears at rehearsals, just so long as she shows up for the performance."

Arthur looked at her blankly. "She is a member of the company just like you, is she not?"

"Indeed she is, and even though she cannot dance a step, I fear that if they had to choose between her and myself, she would get the nod over me."

"But you can dance and very well indeed; I have seen you."

"Thank you, kind sir, but have you seen what it is Phoebe does upon the stage while the rest of the company is hard at work?"

"I do not recall ever noticing her, now that you mention it. But, of course, I had eyes only for you, my dear."

"Quite. Phoebe usually takes a place a little to the side of center stage and stands about during a scene or a number impersonating a statue or an idol or some thing like that. I gather the male members in the audience are quite satisfied if that is all she does."

"Oh, I say! That is a whopper!"

"I tell you it is so. How you can have missed her I cannot begin to imagine, but that is the case with her and must explain to you why it is that she is as free as a bird for most of a rehearsal. I do assure you, if she had to dance but a few steps, it would not go so easy with her."

"I . . . I did not realize, my very dear Charlotte, and I humbly crave your pardon for my lack of understanding."

"I pray you will not look so hangdog, Arthur. There is nothing in it to call for such a lugubrious expression."

"Then you will come out with us on Sunday?"

"I said I would. Where do you have in mind to go?"

"I . . . I thought to keep it as a surprise. It is out away from London."

"Surely not a romp amid the haystacks?" said Charlotte with never a blush.

"N-no, n-not at all," stammered Arthur, blushing for the two of them.

"Might there be a horse to ride when we get there?"

"Er, yes, I daresay, but you are beginning to get it all out of me. It will never be any surprise if you go on," he protested.

"I shall say no more. I have not ridden in years, and it is a good thing you told me this much. I shall go out and order up a habit at once. If it were not so late, I should rush right down and see to it now. I had better inform Phoebe. I am sure she will wish to procure herself a proper dress too."

"I never thought of that."

"Oh, you men! If we have concluded for the evening, I think I should prefer to return home. Tomorrow is bound to be a busy day for me. Securing a comfortable riding habit is not a piece of work to be gone over lightly, and I still have got rehearsals to attend."

"Ah, then you do like the open country?"

"Indeed—at least when there are pleasant things to do and pleasant company to do them with. I think it is the same in the city as in the country, don't you?"

"Yes, of course. I am very pleased that we are in accord upon that score," said Arthur, rising and helping her to her feet. He was more than pleased with himself as he conducted her out of the place.

When Sir Richard and Arthur came to call for the ladies on Sunday in Shadworth's carriage, they were in for something of a surprise. Charlotte looked the picture of a sporting lady as she greeted them at the door of the apartment. Her habit was brandy red from the hem of her sweeping skirt to the very smart little silk topper crowning her burnished locks. Even the wisp of a veil wrapped about the hat had the color, as well as her gloves.

Arthur almost took a step back at the sight, so astonished was he. Sir Richard's eyes widened for a moment and then almost shut as he studied her while she stood, proudly smiling at them, making a simple but graceful gesture of welcome.

Sir Richard was the first to recover himself. He bowed gallantly, then followed Charlotte into the apartment. Arthur was still standing almost completely immobile just without the doorway, only the blinking of his eyes to show he was yet alive.

Sir Richard turned and growled at him, "Coming, Westley?"

Arthur came awake to his state, blushed, and hurried after them.

Once inside, they were in for another shock. Miss Belle was attired in a floral print of a walking dress that was neither in the best of style nor even in good taste. Certainly it was an impossible creation to go with riding.

Sir Richard looked displeased. "Ah, Miss Bell— Phoebe, if I may presume upon our short acquaintance —I beg to inform you that as we are planning to ride this afternoon, your habiliments are not at all suited to that activity."

Phoebe grinned and replied, "Indeed, Sir Richard, as I have never ridden in my life, I did not plan to ride this afternoon; so, as you see, I am appropriately garbed for a stroll in the country."

"Hm . . . yes," said Sir Richard, obviously not happy.

Out of the goodness of her heart, Charlotte suggested, "Dear Sir Richard, I pray you will not be too disappointed if I ride with you and Arthur stays with Phoebe. In that way we shall all have what we wish, shall we not? Arthur, you do not mind at all, do you?"

He most certainly did, but in the face of the charming smile with which she bathed him, he found it impossible to deny her. He put a reasonably good face upon it and acquiesced. Truth be known he had hoped to go about with Charlotte to point out to her the countryside as a husbandman views it, making every attempt to insure her interest in his life's work.

Little more was said. The ladies had packed a picnic lunch and now surrendered the parcels, linen, and crockery to the gentlemen and followed them out to Sir Richard's carriage. There they were handed into the vehicle, the gentlemen following. As the carriage began to roll away, there was a mark of enthusiasm on Sir Richard's countenance that contrasted sharply with the poor expression on Arthur's visage.

CHAPTER NINE

They proceeded in a southwesterly direction, passing through Tothill Field. Charlotte, gazing out of the window, remarked unhappily, "Oh, do not say that it is to Vauxhall Gardens you are taking us."

"Hardly," replied Sir Richard. "We have a deal farther to go than that."

"How much farther?"

"Past Chelsea for starters, my dear. I say, be patient. Sit back and enjoy the drive, We shall be on the road for a spell yet."

Charlotte turned to Phoebe and said lightly, "I do believe we are being abducted."

"Oh, I assure you it is nothing of the sort," said Arthur in all sincerity.

The laughter of the others of the party put him quite out of countenance, and he looked very embarrassed.

Phoebe took his part. "There, now, Mr. Westley, it is quite all right. I mean to say, if this were an abduction, I am sure I should not ask for a handsomer pair of malefactors."

Arthur giggled and the others laughed some more.

The conversation that ensued was the sort of exchange people go through to insure that there will be no uncomfortable silence. There were the usual comments about the weather—it was indeed a very fine day—and about the scenery as they passed out of the more heavily traveled districts that, while not officially a part of London, were peopled by such as could not be styled anything but Londoners.

About midday they stopped at the Chelsea Bun House for a delightful repast, after which Sir Richard encouraged them all by informing them that they would arrive at their destination within the hour. This news, added to the excellent meal, raised their spirits, and the atmosphere in the carriage, as they continued on, was appreciably merrier than it had been.

Sir Richard's word was good, and just short of an hour later they drove through the gates of a very handsome estate on the outskirts of Fulham.

"This is Curlingame House, a residence of the Earl of Hayford," Shadworth told them. "The family is not in residence at the moment, but I have free access, as I keep some of my hunters here. Naturally it is too far to go, all the way up to Melton Mowbray, if I have a wish for a ride in the country. The earl, long a friend of the family, graciously consented to making his stables available to my stock. We are free to ride over the entire estate."

Arthur was craning his neck to survey the lands as they drove up the drive and then turned out of it, heading for the stables.

"Oh, look!" cried Phoebe, very excited. "They have got a farm! Oh, please may we not go through the barns and see the animals? I have never seen a farm before."

"Why, that would be an excellent idea!" exclaimed Sir Richard, with sudden inspiration. "I have no doubt that our eminent agriculturist, Mr. Arthur Westley, would be only too happy to oblige you in the matter while Charlotte and I try the mettle of my mounts."

"Indeed yes, Phoebe," agreed Charlotte. "I think it would be a very fine thing. Arthur, I am sure you will not hesitate to do the honors for Miss Bell."

Arthur was sure he would have, rather; but, even though resentment filled his breast, he knew that he could not refuse, and gracefully accepted the charge. When they dismounted from the carriage at the stable, he had not even a chance to make some sort of farewell gesture to Charlotte, for Phoebe took him by the arm and, as great a fellow as he was, whisked him along with her, heading for a building that had the appearance of a dairy.

Charlotte watched them go and smiled. She turned to Sir Richard and remarked, "I am so relieved. I had no idea how Phoebe would spend her time, since she cannot ride. How very clever of you, Sir Richard, to have arranged an outing to this place. Now both Phoebe and Arthur will be vastly entertained, I am sure."

"I pray, Charlotte, that you, too, will have a jolly afternoon, with me for company, out upon the bridle paths."

"Never doubt it, dear sir. I had long given up hope of ever sitting upon a good horse again. I venture to guess that I have not been out riding in a dozen years— not since I was a governess for the Walkhams. They kept a pony for their children."

"Hmmm . . yes, of course. If you will take my arm, I shall escort you to the paddock where our mounts are waiting," he said, not looking at her as he offered his arm. The tone of his voice was distant.

Charlotte immediately understood that her having been a governess was not one of the things about her that appealed to him. She resolved to keep her past out of their conversation.

The horse was a darling and the saddle was a delight. Obviously there had been some improvements in ladies' saddles since last she had ridden. Instead of harsh pegs to drape her limbs over, they were now softly padded, and there was not any of that preliminary shifting about to find a comfortable position. Why, with such a saddle, she was sure she could ride all day without experiencing the least strain.

Charlotte never waited for Sir Richard to get mounted but urged her horse into a gallop and sailed away out of the paddock.

Sir Richard, one foot in the stirrup, stared at her and forgot to get up on his horse. Slowly he disengaged his foot and stood against the saddle, studying the flying figures of Charlotte and her horse. "I say," he said aloud, "boil me if that is not the finest seat on a female I have ever seen. I cannot believe she has not ridden in years." Suddenly he turned to the grooms standing about: "Here, what is the delay? I say, the lady is in the next county and I am still standing here, what?"

The stablemen, understanding this complaint as a call for assistance, rushed to help Sir Richard up on his horse. Irritably he slapped them away:

"Get out of it, you perishing fools! I do not need your bloody help!" Even as he exploded, he went up lightly into the saddle and spurred his horse into a headlong dash after Charlotte.

A half-hour had gone by and they were still in the dairy. Arthur had no sense of time, for he was speaking on his favorite subject and to a most appreciative audience. Phoebe was as full of questions as an admiring child, and it was Arthur's very sincere and great pleasure to respond to them in the fullest detail. In fact, he was very nearly ecstatic, as for the past year he had had to hold his peace in the society he frequented or be labeled a bore.

At first, because her questions were so utterly childish, he had thought that she was putting on an act with him. He had tried to be offhanded in his answers, but this never satisfied her, and she kept at him until the gates of his knowledge and expertise burst and he began to talk with an enthusiasm he had never been able to indulge with anyone before.

After they had done with the dairy, Phoebe dragged him out to the hen house and once again assaulted him with a barrage of questions. And so it went until a husbandman on the estate came up and offered to show them about. Arthur refused his services but asked him for a description of how the fields were planted and managed. In the ensuing discussion the husbandman forgot the attractions of the lady—which had prompted his kind offer in the first place—and stayed to listen to Arthur expound on his theories of farming. In a little while other hands came to hear him, and even Lord Hayford's farm manager—in former days his steward—came out of the great house to investigate the little crowd and stayed to join the discussion.

Phoebe was delighted and not a little impressed with the way all these grand retainers of an earl hearkened to Arthur. While she did not know a thing about it, she was tremendously interested. To hear firsthand from an expert, who happened to be a very attractive gentleman into the bargain, how things were made to grow and to produce such ordinary but necessary things as the cheese and eggs and bacon she had every morning for breakfast was quite a revelation to her. It was so different from the rough ways of the fishermen who wrested their wares from the briny deep and hauled them into Billingsgate to be sold. Indeed, this husbandry was a deal more complicated but no less interesting for that. Oh, how she would have loved to live on a farm!

Sir Richard and Charlotte came riding back to the paddock side by side. Charlotte had a glowing look about her and had never appeared more beautiful. Sir

Richard must have thought so, for he never took his eyes from her face and was gallant and gentle to a degree while helping her out of the saddle.

"My girl, you ride like a dream—and something of a devil, too. Few men could have put me to such effort to stay up with them."

"You are too flattering, Sir Richard," said Charlotte, smiling graciously at him. Then her expression turned to consternation as Phoebe and Arthur came up to them. "For heaven's sake, Phoebe, what has happened? Did you fall? It is a mercy, then, that you did not try to ride. Arthur, what have you been up to to permit my friend to appear in such a wretched state?" She went over to the beaming Phoebe and began to rub some of the filth from her cheeks. "This is disgraceful, Phoebe! Were you hurt badly?"

Phoebe grinned. "It is nothing, nothing at all, and do not lay it at Mr. Westley's doorstep, either. He was most kind. Do you know he is a veritable fount of knowledge about growing things and had his lordship's hands spellbound for hours. It is nothing. I tell you. I slipped and fell when we climbed down an embankment about one of the fields. It was planted in beans. Did you know that they had the prettiest flowers?"

Charlotte tried to speak, but Phoebe was full of her afternoon and kept right on:

"And we saw the dearest little lambs! Oh, I do think I have quite lost my appetite for chops. They are so very cuddlesome."

"Phoebe, what has come over you?" demanded Charlotte, highly irked. "Have you never been to a farm before that you should make such an unladylike fuss about such inconsequentialities?"

"I told you I had not. I never dreamed it could be so interesting——"

"Enough! Sir Richard, is there someplace I may take my friend to make her more presentable? Without a glass, she cannot comprehend how wretched is her appearance."

"Of course. Let us repair to the house. I imagine they will offer us some refreshment as well."

The two gentlemen awaited their lady friends in a small drawing room, where they were served some excellent brandy. Sir Richard was enjoying his—it was just the thing after his equestrian exercises—but Arthur was frowning and staring at his glass as though he hated it.

"I say, that Charlotte can surely ride," declared Sir Richard heartily. "You never told me she could."

"I did not know it myself," growled Arthur.

Sir Richard turned to him with a frown. "Here, now, what's this? Are you in the mopes? Was not Miss Bell pleasant company?"

"I have nothing to say against Miss Bell. She is a delightful creature, a very entertaining companion, but——"

" 'Entertaining'? May I inquire precisely what you mean by that?" asked Sir Richard, beginning to bristle.

"Now, what the devil has got *you* up in the boughs? You seemed to be having a high time of it with *my* lady."

"I was thinking that you were not so unhappy at being left with *my* lady," retorted Sir Richard.

"I'd not have been left with your lady if you had not dreamed up this nonsensical business in the first place. What have we proved, I ask you? Your lady could not care less for horses, whereas mine appears to dote on them. If that has any meaning at all, I say I have won the wager. Miss Lequesne is a horsewoman, which is a step to being quite at home in the country. To put a point on it, Shadworth, I believe you owe me five hundred."

"You are out in your thinking, Westley. A horsewoman is not a farm creature. Why, that girl could be up with the leaders in any chase, and you know that the hunt is a far cry from farming. She'd ride your turnip crops ragged, by Jove. Damn! If she was anything but a stage trollope, she could fit into the highest society in Melton country *or* in London."

"How dare you, sir! She is a lady despite the trade she follows, and I am willing to prove that fact upon you with any weapon you care to name!"

"Here now, do not go hot under the collar so quickly. Let us talk this out. It would be a nasty business if we were to come to quarreling over the likes of *her.*"

"There you go again, impugning the lady who some-day shall be my wife. I have never regretted anything so much as this wretched outing! Shadworth, either you will regard my lady with the respect that is her due or you and I shall have more than words together."

"But be reasonable, man! Think of what will be said of you. To wed a female of the stage? That is most exceptional and you know it."

Arthur cooled down and nodded. "Aye, I am aware of what will be said. But it would be only at the beginning. When they see her, when they come to know her, they will also come to understand what a gem I found."

"Bah! There is more to it than that. After London, do you think a woman like that can have any wish to settle down upon a great farm? I say not! She was never meant for it. She is far better suited to a chap like myself. I have been speaking with her and I know her tastes march a deal closer with mine than they do with yours. Actually, it occurred to me that we ought to trade. You take Phoebe and I take Charlotte."

"The very thought of Miss Lequesne in your arms is revolting to me, Shadworth. You have not the least appreciation of her worth. I am having to hold on to my temper to even discuss the matter with you. Now, I pray you will cease your unhappy comments and tell me what more we have to do to settle this business."

"What business?"

"The wager."

Sir Richard shrugged. "It is settled, as far as I am concerned. I never thought she was a proper female for you in the first place. It is up to you to prove she is. This trip has proved it quite my way, if it has proved anything at all."

"Then it appears that we shall never settle it until I wed her. In that case, I suggest that we forget the business entirely and devote ourselves to the lady of our choice, and to hell with these bloody outings of yours!"

Again Sir Richard shrugged. "It is quite all right with me, although I do not see the harm if we were to come out again for another day like today."

"Not on your life if you think to go riding with Charlotte again. The next time, you stay with Phoebe and I shall take Charlotte out. I am no laggard when it comes to a good horse, my friend."

"I suggest we both take Charlotte out and leave Phoebe home. I prefer a good hearty ride to a dreary chat about nonsense any day."

"That is the silliest arrangement I have ever heard. You stay with Phoebe and I stay with Charlotte and that is final. If you have a wish to come along, then teach Phoebe to ride. I am sure you could find a deal of pleasure in it. She is not exactly plain, you know."

"I cannot leave you alone with Miss Lequesne. I have taken it as a solemn duty not to allow you to make an ass of yourself over the lady."

"Who in bloody blazes ever asked you to!"

Sir Richard grinned impudently at him. "I told you *I* have taken it upon myself, and furthermore, I have a great desire to go out riding with Charlotte again. Really, old chap, it would be so much less of a bother if you acquiesced in the exchange I suggested."

Arthur sneered at him. "Even if I did not hold her in the highest regard, I should never surrender her to the likes of *you,* you chaser of skirts."

Sir Richard guffawed. "Aren't we all," he replied, and laughed some more.

"Oh, hush you! I believe they are coming."

Charlotte and Phoebe came into the room, looking quite refreshed and happy. It was obvious that they were enjoying themselves.

Charlotte sailed over to Sir Richard and took him by the hands, exclaiming, "Oh, Sir Richard, it has been a most delightful outing! I pray you will forward my thanks and gratitude to Lord Hayford. I wish we could do it again; I do so like to ride."

"But of course we shall then," replied Sir Richard. "As soon again as you wish, and as often, my dear."

Phoebe clapped her hands together and turned to Arthur, saying, "I should just love it, Mr. Westley! I am sure we have not seen a half of the farm and it is all so very interesting."

Since Arthur was blinking with uncertainty, Sir Richard thought to help him by saying, "Of course you would be delighted, wouldn't you, Westley?"

As Arthur had no choice, he said, "Indeed, Miss Bell, it would be my pleasure to show you about again."

At which point Sir Richard exploded with laughter despite the fact that Arthur was looking daggers at him.

CHAPTER TEN

"Miss Faulconer, the ladies will not rise," declared the older of Nancy's maids, a disapproving look upon her face.

"I imagine they came in very late last night. Well, I shall see what I can do. In the meantime, lay out my third-best walking dress, the Isabella. I am not in a colorful mood this day."

She left and went into Charlotte's bedchamber. It was quite apparent the woman had accomplished nothing with Charlotte, for her repose was completely undisturbed. Nancy went over to her and shook her vigorously by the shoulder. "Come, you slugabed! Rehearsals are on in an hour."

Charlotte waved an arm and murmured, "Go away. Wake me when the others are up."

"Charlotte, this is Nancy! Now do you arise from your bed at once! Good heavens, how late were you out last night? You know today is a day for hard work."

"Oh . . . it's you, Nancy." Charlotte slowly arose to a sitting position and yawned and stretched. "Is it late?"

"It will be if you do not get to moving, Miss Lequesne. Tell me, how did things go with your gentlemen yesterday?" Nancy took a seat as Charlotte began her toilet.

"Oh, we had a very nice time. It was quite the most pleasant day I have spent in years."

Nancy smiled. "Ah . . . then Mr. Westley has begun to improve himself in your eyes."

"Who? Arthur? No, of course not! Well, I mean to say, it was nothing like that at all. It was . . . well, it was a bit complicated."

"Oh, dear, then you had best save it. Dear Phoebe is not out of bed yet and I must see to her, not that the Opera House would collapse if she never turned up for rehearsals. Still, she might as well pretend, at least, that she is a part of the company."

Nancy left and entered Phoebe's room, only to find that Phoebe had already risen and was well on her way to completing her dressing. In fact, she must have been in excellent spirits, for she was singing, and Phoebe could never carry a tune.

"Oh, bless you, Nancy! I had hoped to have a word with you this morning. Do you think I ought to marry a farmer?"

Nancy stared at her, taken completely by surprise. "You, Phoebe, a farmer's wife? Well, I never! I thought surely you were setting your cap for a duke or, at the very least, an earl."

"Little one, I am serious. Those gents are all right to have a bit of fun with every now and again, but I never took any of them seriously. I should have been thrice a fool to listen to their promises and blandishments. I mean to say, I took whatever they offered and will continue to do so for as long as I am not otherwise occupied, but Charlotte and I went out to Fulham yesterday, and there was the most *beautiful* farm. I say, have you ever visited a farm?"

"I have seen gardens in the City, but no, I have never set foot outside London."

"Oh, you should! It is nothing at all like the City. Why do you not have Lord Faile take you out sometime? I am sure you will love it. As for me, I have made up my mind. After I have done with the ballet, I shall settle down upon a farm. I daresay I shall have to marry a farmer to do that."

"I daresay," said Nancy, not quite sure she was hearing it all correctly. She recovered herself and inquired, "But what of Sir Richard Shadworth? You *were* out with him, were you not?"

"Oh, yes."

"But he is a sportsman. What would he be doing visiting a farm?"

"Oh, he went off with Charlotte and I stayed behind with Mr. Westley, who explained everything about the place. That is a very knowledgeable gentleman, Nancy. One would never think it to look at him, but he knows more about farming than all of Lord Hayford's husbandmen put together."

"Lord Hayford?" asked Nancy faintly.

"I shall tell you all about it at breakfast. I say, you have not eaten yet, have you? I am as hungry as a horse and I should so much like your company. I have so much to tell you! How is it with Lord Faile these days?"

Nancy shrugged the question away and said, "You did say that Charlotte went off with Sir Richard, did you not? I do not think that Mr. Westley could have been overjoyed at that outcome."

"Oh, he was quite sweet about it and spent his time with me."

Nancy raised a hand to her troubled brow and murmured, "Yes, we must talk at breakfast. Do hurry. Between you and Charlotte, I am not sure if I got up this morning. Things are in a bit of a muddle, it appears to me."

Phoebe laughed. "Not a bit, my dear. It is all very smooth indeed, and we shall be repeating the experience shortly. Sir Richard has promised."

"But what does Mr. Westley say to it?"

"He was a perfect dear. He was delighted, of course."

Almost everything Nancy did in the theater these days was a premier performance for the reason that so much of her dancing was now done *en pointe*. The rehearsal she was just finishing with Jack Clack was another such. It would be the first time the part of Juliet had been danced upon the very tips of the ballerina's toes.

It was first for another reason. Actually the ballet was an interlude between acts of the Georg Antonin Benda opera *Romeo und Julia*. As an opera, it was not particularly noteworthy, and in English translation, perhaps even less so. Dr. Crawford, the director of music, had laughed Bouquin to scorn when the signor had suggested the work be performed, but his opposition had been routed when Bouquin explained that he had an idea for a ballet, featuring Miss Faulconer as Juliet, that would "make of the performance a jewel in the diadem of Terpsichore no matter what opera was performed. . . ." He then went on to enlarge upon his conception and immediately won Mr. Coates to his side. Dr. Crawford grumbled agreement on the condition that he cut parts of the work out so as not to insult his singers and the audience. This marched right along with Signor Bouquin's wishes, and he immediately began to plan an even longer interlude.

The first full run-through of the ballet was proving a great delight to almost everyone in the theater. Only one party was not overly happy with it, and he was not a part of the company. He was sitting in his box, an observer, watching with a strained expression the simulated lovemaking between the dancers. He had to admit it was being beautifully done; still, it was rubbing him raw.

To great applause from her colleagues standing about on the stage, Nancy bowed out into the emptiness of the theater. Then, smiling with gratitude, she turned and executed *révérences* to her fellow performers on the three sides of the stage.

By the time she had done, Lord Faile had descended from his box and come striding out from the wings. He snatched up a towel and carried it to Nancy, throwing it about her shoulders. Then, taking her by the arm, he led her off into the wings.

"But, my lord, I am not done!" she protested. "I have got to confer with Dr. Crawford and Clack. There is a part that may have to be rewritten. The tempo is not quite right, you see."

"It is quite all right; I am sure they will wait for you. I would speak with you about this latest creation of Bouquin's. I am not so sure that I approve."

But Nancy was not listening. Her head came up and there was a bright smile on her face as she asked, "My lord, do you think you could arrange it so that we might visit a farm?"

"Nancy, you are not heeding—— A *farm?* Of course I can arrange it, but why in the world should you wish to visit a farm?'

"Phoebe says it is quite the most wonderful thing she has ever seen. I have never been to see a farm," she ended sadly.

"Are you sure you know what you are asking? I suspect that Miss Bell's olfactory sense is not what it ought to be by reason of her earlier associations with noisome Billingsgate, but, my dear, I would point out to you that your pretty little nose is bound to be offended. A poorly managed farm can be a bit of a foul hell, my word upon it."

"Oh, but this place is not at all like that."

"What place do you refer to?"

"It is in Fulham, an estate of a Lord Hayford. Are you by any chance acquainted with the nobleman?"

"How do you come to know Hayford?" inquired Tony. "That is quite an exclusive circle he moves in."

"Oh, I do not know anything at all about the gentleman. It is Phoebe——"

"Phoebe! How on God's earth does *she* come to know Lord Hayford?"

"Truly, my lord, there is nothing in it so bad as to get your wind up."

"I beg your pardon, but it came as a bit of a shock to me. I mean to say, we both know that Phoebe is no better than she should be."

"Tony Faile, I resent your remark! You ought to be ashamed to cast aspersions on a poor Billingsgate creature who has managed to rise to some of the highest gentlemen in the land and has, for months now, got them to dangle after her for hardly anything but her company in return."

Tony cocked his head at Nancy. There was a little smile flickering about his lips as he asked, "I say, is that true?"

"It most certainly is. Phoebe is a deal smarter than most. In the company of bucks like you, she manages to hide it quite well, I think."

Tony burst into laughter. "My dear, in the future, I shall take my hat off to Phoebe, both literally and figuratively. Hmmm, I think I should like to know her better."

"Be careful, my lord, or she will have you, too, added to her line of puppies."

A warm light came into his eyes as he responded,

"Never a chance, my sweet. The gossips have me assigned to the line that follows you about."

"A line? But there is no line, Tony. You are the only one."

He sighed. "Too true, and one would hope that I would fare better than Phoebe's poor bucks."

"Tony, I must return to the company. I am sure that they are waiting for me."

"It begins to appear that I have got to look up the earl of Hayford and arrange a visit for you."

"Oh, it is so good of you to oblige me, but it will not be necessary for you to go to any trouble at all. Sir Richard Shadworth is going to arrange it. I do so want to go. Will you speak with him?"

"Shadworth? How well do you know Shadworth? He does not have a very nice reputation. Nancy, I do not wish for you to mix with unsavory characters. Heaven knows but your work brings you into contact with more than a sufficiency of them."

"Too true. It was my work that brought me to *your* notice, my lord," said Nancy pointedly.

"*Touché!*" he cried with a laugh. "But, pray how do you come to know this Shadworth?"

"But I do not *know* him, Tony. You met him at the apartment one evening. He is Phoebe's escort these days."

Tony chuckled. "Excellent . . . most excellent. Now, there is a cold fish I should like to see hooked. My blessings to Phoebe. From what you say, she is the proper female for him. Oh, very well, I shall look up Shadworth and see what he has to say."

Nancy clapped her hands and cried, 'Oh, thank you, Tony! I do like you so very much!" On tiptoes, she reached up and kissed him on the cheek. Then she quickly ran off back to the stage.

Lord Faile stared after. "Am I some sort of idiot?

Am I any better than any of the other bucks hanging about in the lobby?"

For a moment he pondered the proposition. Finally he shook his head doubtfully and murmured to himself: "I wonder."

It was all quite easily arranged. Lord Faile sent round a note to Sir Richard, asking him to call and share a brandy with him. Sir Richard was only too happy to oblige the Marquis. Although neither counted the other as more than an acquaintance, Lord Faile knew Sir Richard by his reputation as a sportsman, and everyone who was anyone was quite pleased to brag of the Marquis of Faile's notice.

The two gentlemen got along rather well, considering their differing temperaments, and another outing to Lord Hayford's estate in Fulham was easily agreed upon.

Immediately, Sir Richard sent off an express to his absentee host, and by return post Lord Faile received a confirming invitation from the earl to make free of his estate, together with an apology that were it not for family matters that demanded his presence at his family seat in Berkshire, he would have been exceedingly pleased to welcome my lord marquis in person.

The day appointed for the outing arrived and two carriages departed London, the one in the lead, as before, carrying Sir Richard, Arthur Westley, Charlotte, and Phoebe; the one behind, Tony and Nancy.

In the normal course of events, an outing comprised of three couples would have been no cause for comment, but Lord Hayford happened to mention it to Lady Hayford, and she in turn happened to mention it in a letter she had just sent to her sister in London, so that immediately the fashionable world was agog with the news. Many looked down their noses at the spectacle of three men and their mistresses going out to visit the countryside; nor did they think very highly of Lord Hayford for lending his estate to such an unsavory purpose. It is extremely doubtful that one could have found a single soul in London who believed the purpose of the trip was purely innocent.

La Belle Bell had made a notorious name for herself among the theater bucks for being fast. Sir Richard Shadworth was fast and would have been the last one to have denied it.

As for Lord Faile, there was something respectful in society's regard of him. At least, he had never been known to have more than one mistress at a time, and those who had seen Miss Faulconer practicing her art upon the stage of the Opera House were inclined to be something envious of the nobleman, for she was a graceful and pretty young thing. That is, the gentlemen might have felt that way about it, but the ladies saw nothing good in the business at all. As for Miss Lequesne and Arthur Westley, one could judge them by the company they kept.

Of course, no one was brave enough to make any criticism likely to reach the ears of Lord Faile, and so the little party went off into the sunshine that held sway beyond the confines of fumy London, light of heart and carefree of reputation.

At the end of the day, as the two carriages wended their way back to London, everyone had had a good time, even Arthur—although he would have been the last one to admit it. Just as on the previous visit to Fulham, Charlotte and Sir Richard went riding off together, leaving him to entertain Phoebe as best he could, which, by Phoebe's estimate, was very well indeed. He continued with her education in husbandry, and she was lost in an admiration well laced with a genuine interest in what he had to say—and in himself as well.

Tony and Nancy tagged along with them for a bit, but their interest never matched Phoebe's, so that in a little while, filled to repletion with planting schedules and methods of properly storing the great variety of harvest crops, they went about on their own until Tony decided that Nancy should have her first riding lesson.

Nancy was not particularly thrilled at his suggestion, and as she drew near to the beast that was to bear her, the prospect grew quiet daunting. Tony had arranged for her to borrow appropriate toggery from the wardrobes of the daughters of the earl's household, and as they were not at all petite, Nancy was like to drown in the habit that was finally assembled for her. This added nothing to her self-confidence, but it sent Tony off into roars of appreciative laughter. So grateful was he for her affording him such a mirthful sight that he had to plant a very warm kiss upon her lips as he lifted her up in his arms and deposited her into the saddle. Then there followed a most embarrassing time as Tony had to describe precisely how she was to arrange her one limb about the pegs and bear her weight on the other foot resting in the one stirrup. The grooms standing about found it all excruciatingly funny, and Tony did not help matters a bit by being short with them while he winked his eye. Nancy saw all this and found it a deal more comical than she would have admitted.

As they were traveling home, Tony remarked, "My dear, you have an excellent seat—or would have if only you would exert yourself to control the beast. It is a fact that the rider commands his beast and not the other way about."

"Oh, but he was such a *great* beast, I did not feel up to debating with him. In any event, I had no objection to going where he wished."

Tony found that to be very funny, quite worthy of a warm salute upon the lips that left them both breathless. The drive back to her apartment was filled with nonsensical little episodes like that, so that the pair of them were in excellent spirits as they took leave of each other.

The other carriage came right up after them to deposit Charlotte and Phoebe at their doorstep, and Sir Richard took the opportunity to thank Charlotte in much the same fashion as Tony had done with Nancy.

Arthur was about to protest when two strong hands turned him right about and he was engulfed in Phoebe's caress. He would have been hard put to say how it happened, but he discovered himself returning her kiss with an ardor he had thought was reserved only for Charlotte.

CHAPTER ELEVEN

The next morning, the three ladies were all in a jolly humor as they partook of a hearty breakfast of fresh eggs, fresh bacon, and fresh butter, all from the Hayford estate, which only served to make the buns from the local bakeshop something less than fresh by comparison.

"I should like to wed," remarked Phoebe out of a clear blue sky.

Both Nancy and Charlotte turned to her good-humoredly but with looks of disbelief on their countenances.

"Just like that?" asked Charlotte. "Of course, you have someone in mind, no doubt?"

Phoebe regarded her with a shrewd look. "I might. It strikes me that I am doing myself little good with the gentlemen of the lobby. I shall never meet any sort of a farming gentleman there."

Charlotte said, "Oh, but you have. Arthur is certainly that. In fact, if I had any complaint to make of the gentleman, it is that he is only that. He is filled with his farm in Leicestershire until I could scream from the sheer boredom of it. Now, you take Sir Richard. *He* has entree into the most genteel society. If I had any complaint to make of *him,* it would be of his neglect of his social obligations. I mean to say, Sir Richard has a part to play in society. He is quite a most fashionable gentleman, you will have to admit. The sporting world is all well and good for a gentleman, but there are other, more important things in life that ought not to be neglected."

"Odd, I could not care less about that sort of thing," said Phoebe.

Charlotte bit her tongue rather than retort that it was to be expected of a Billingsgate cit. Instead she said, "It appears to me that you have found a great deal to interest you in Mr. Westley, and as we are all agreed, he is the personification of an agriculturist."

Phoebe chuckled. "Amazing coincidence, by Jove! As a matter of fact, I am beginning to think that you, my dear Charlotte, do not particularly care for the gentleman—in any serious way, that is."

Charlotte smiled. "As a matter of fact, my dear Phoebe, I was coming to a similar conclusion with regard to you and Sir Richard. He is not more to you than any other of your many gentleman friends, is he?"

"Dearest Charlotte, you are quite correct in your thinking."

"I am so pleased to know it."

"Oh, for heaven's sake! Why, then, do you not trade partners with each other?" exclaimed Nancy.

Charlotte turned to look at her sweetly. "She is such a dear child."

"And clever, too," added Phoebe, as sweetly.

Nancy looked from one to the other, nonplussed for a moment, and then she smiled. "Ah—that was what you had in mind all the time!"

Phoebe nodded with overdrawn satisfaction. "Did I not say the dear little thing was quite clever?"

All three then put their heads together to discuss in what manner the exchange could be accomplished. The surprising thing about the ensuing conversation was that it never took into account the feelings of the gentlemen under discussion.

For Sir Richard, the previous day's events had been invigorating for more than one reason, and he had slept soundly and well—so well that his repose was come to an end well before his usual hour of rising and he was down to breakfast before Arthur had finished his, a most singular happening.

He entered the little room that served for breakfast and perused the latest journals, with a hearty greeting for his guest, then took his seat at the table, where Tompkins began to serve him. To his surprise, for it was obvious that Arthur was in the midst of his morning meal, that gentleman threw down his serviette with a broad gesture of anger, rose, and began to stalk out of the room.

"Westley, what's this?" asked Sir Richard, as much puzzled as surprised.

Arthur wheeled about and declared, "I beg to inform you, sir, that I am leaving this house at once!"

"Why, where the deuce are you off to?"

"That, sir, is not any of your bloody business!"

"At a guess, I should say that you are in a pet about something. Since it cannot involve me, I bid you speak up, old chap, and make your complaint. I shall see it is attended to at once. Your eggs are too cold?"

"A pet? Ha, ha!" laughed Arthur hollowly. "We shall see what sort of a pet it is when my seconds come to call!"

"Your seconds? Don't be a perishing idiot! Come back to the table and finish your breakfast. By God, the eggs *are* cold now. Tompkins, more eggs for Mr. Westley."

"I do not want your bloody eggs."

"You were bloody well gobbling them down when I came in."

"Precisely, sir! When you came in, I lost my bloody appetite."

"Will you sit down before I knock you down? I haven't a clue as to what is eating at your gizzard, and you owe me an explanation here and now or, by God, it will be *my* seconds calling upon *you,* blast you!"

"Very well, although I truly doubt you could. Perhaps I owe you an explanation, but you owe me a damn sight more!"

As Arthur sat himself down and began to attack the cold eggs, Tompkins came up with a pair of fresh hot ones off the steamer. When he saw that Mr. Westley was working on the cold ones, he started to turn away, but Arthur reached out a long arm to hold him fast, and as his mouth was full, he had to gesture for him to deposit the eggs next to his plate. Tompkins did so and went back to the buffet.

In the meantime, Sir Richard had taken a few sips from his cup while he stared at his friend and guest. Then his eyes lit up and he said accusingly, "It's the blasted wager that has got you up in the boughs, isn't it."

"It's a deal more than that, but that is as good a place to start with as any."

"I tell you I am not paying a penny until it is clear that you have won it. At this point in time, I do not see that you have proven a thing. By the way, what were you supposed to be at proving, anyway?"

Arthur frowned as he racked his brain. "It had something to do with Charlotte, I believe."

"Great Jupiter, do you think I don't know that much? Precisely *what* were you supposed to do about her?"

"Ah, I've got it! I was supposed to show you that she

is fit to be my wife, and you never gave me a chance to prove anything with her. That was awfully low of you. You took every advantage of her love for riding to quite cut me out with her."

"I did nothing of the kind. It was obvious to me the lady preferred my company to yours. She never demurred in the slightest to riding out with me."

"Only because I was never given a chance to ask her!"

"What the devil are you complaining about? You seemed to have spent all your time out there with La Belle Bell. Are you claiming that *that* lovely is not worthy of your time?"

"I am not claiming anything of the sort, but it has nothing to do——"

"You do not dislike the lady, do you?"

"No, of course I do not dislike——"

"In fact, when you come to think on it, you might say you like the lady very much."

Arthur first shook his head in frustration, then nodded it in affirmation. "Yes, yes, I like her very much, but I still say that that has nothing to say to it."

"It has a great deal to say to it, you ass! I think the lady likes *you* very much. Damn if she ever hung on my arm the way she hung on yours."

"Piffle! The fact remains that Charlotte is mine, and you have no business to cut me out!" declared Arthur.

"The devil you say! First of all, she certainly is not yours, and second, all's fair in love and war."

"That is piffle, sir."

"Piffle yourself, sir!" retorted Sir Richard.

"That is my word, sir. Go find your own."

"Very well, it is all twaddle," said Sir Richard.

"Then you agree with me."

"I agree that you are filled with twaddle," retorted Sir Richard.

For a moment Arthur looked blank. "Oh, I say, I have quite lost the thread. Where are we?"

Sir Richard looked up to the ceiling pleadingly. "Arthur, I think you need a keeper. Have you any idea of what it is you are trying to say?"

"But of course I do. Until you took us quite off the track, I was about to warn you to stay clear of Charlotte. I intend to make her my wife."

"Oh, now I do recall. I bet you a monkey you'd never manage it."

"And I am claiming that you are taking every unfair advantage to prevent my even trying. I mean to say, if I am never to be alone with her, how can I begin to proceed?"

Sir Richard looked at him and took a bite of his egg absentmindedly. He made a face and threw his spoon down. *"Pfaugh!* These perishing eggs are cold! Westley, cannot you let a man eat his breakfast in peace? Tompkins, more eggs!"

"I beg pardon, sir, but Mr. Westley consumed the last."

Sir Richard glared at Arthur. "Just for that, I ought to challenge you to a meeting at dawn. Egad but you are a sore trial to me this morning! When do you have it in mind to depart for Leicestershire?"

"I am leaving this house upon the instant, but I shall not be leaving for Leicestershire until I have got me a wife to keep me company on the trip."

"It will never be Charlotte."

"You have already said as much and it makes no difference to me."

Sir Richard shook his head. "My dear Westley, I see that for as long as you have this bee in your bonnet, there is no talking with you, but until you come to your senses, one way or another, you will continue to be my guest. For heaven's sake, man, think of my reputation!

How would it look if a dear friend of mine refused my hospitality after enjoying it for over a year?"

"I daresay it would look rather.bad for you."

"It would look quite bad for both of us, especially if it ever got out that we were quarreling about two light-skirts from the ballet."

Arthur stood up. He was in quite a temper now. "Shadworth, you have now gone too far! You have impugned my lady's name! Dare you to assert that Miss Lequesne carried herself in a manner unbecoming a lady at any time with you?"

"No, she did not. All right, I apologize. Come to think of it, except that she is in the ballet, there is nothing to say against her."

"You appear to forget it quickly enough. This is not the first time we have had this argument," Arthur pointed out.

Sir Richard nodded. "Yes, I agree with you. Miss Lequesne is not what one expects from the ballet. Hmmm . . ."

"What are you thinking?" inquired Arthur.

"I am thinking that with her excellent seat, she could quite hold her own in *my* set. Oh well, it is just a thought. I say, have you anything on this morning?"

"No. Why?"

"I thought you and I could go down to the club and look in."

Arthur shook his head. "I am not about to leave these premises until we have reached a settlement."

Absently Sir Richard took up another bit of egg. Again he made a face. "Damn! They are even colder than before. I say, Tompkins, surely there is some hot coffee about."

"Very good, sir." Tompkins filled a fresh cup and brought it over.

Sir Richard took a sip and sighed. "Aye, that is better. I was like to freeze my liver."

"Well?" asked Arthur.

"Well, what?" replied Sir Richard.

"I am asking you, what are we going to do with Charlotte?"

"We? I beg your pardon, but *we* are not going to do anything about the lady. It is strictly a matter of every man for himself."

"But your intentions are not honorable!" accused Arthur, "I will not have it!"

"It is never a question what *you* will have, old chap. It is quite up to the lady in question, I think."

"In any case, I am going to ask her to marry me," declared Arthur.

"Bully for you! But it says nothing to how she may respond to your offer."

Arthur looked uncertain. "If you know something, I pray you will spit it out."

"I do not know a thing except for the fact that I have a liking for the lady."

"I do not trust you, Shadworth."

Sir Richard laughed. "You are well-advised not to, old friend."

Arthur got up and began to pace the floor. Finally he stopped and, turning to Sir Richard, raised a finger, which he shook as he declared solemnly, "Only blood can settle it between us."

"Oh, I say! We have just established that it would look rather queer if you removed yourself to other quarters. And, I say! We can hardly conduct the preliminaries of an affair of honor when we are living together. I mean to say, are you going out to have your seconds come calling on me. It would be unheard of for you to be present at the negotiations. It isn't done, you know. By the way, I imagine you may not have anyone about in London to serve. I shall lend you a friend or two of my own, if you like."

"Shadworth, you are not taking this at all seriously. I assure you you will live to regret it."

"Thank you; I am relieved to know it. Regretfully or not, I am pleased to know that I shall survive the outcome of the affair."

Arthur turned and looked at him blankly. "What are you talking about?"

"You said I shall *live* to regret it, old man. I am pleased to know that it will not be to the death."

Arthur snorted. "You know damn well what I mean."

"Oh, very well; as you are my guest, I am honor bound to humor you. Whom will you choose to act for you?"

"Not any of *your* friends, you may be sure."

"All right, whom have you got?" demanded Sir Richard.

"I shall find someone," retorted Arthur doggedly. "What weapons shall it be?"

"Why talk of weapons?" demanded Sir Richard. "That is for the seconds to come to terms upon. So you see, if you have not got seconds, you may not fight a duel. I hope that settles the business."

"Not on your life! I know a gentleman you would find quite unexceptional. *He* shall be my second."

"Whom do you know that I would not take exception to?"

Arthur, very sure of himself, said, "A gentleman who has no greater acquaintance with you than he has with me."

Sir Richard frowned. "I say, you do not mean to—— No, you cannot mean it! Only my Lord Faile fits the case. Surely you do not intend to bring so eminent a gentleman into our petty squables. He is a marquis, man!"

"I am sure that, in an affair of honor, my Lord Faile must prove acceptable to you."

Sir Richard brought a great fist crashing down upon the table, rattling the tableware and making Tompkins start, his eyes popping open wide. "No! I say no! I have put up with enough of this nonsense, and this is nonsense beyond anything. You shall not approach his lordship in the matter. I absolutely forbid it!"

"Hah!" Arthur was smiling now that he had got Sir Richard hot with anger. "And, pray, how can you stop me—by challenging me to a duel? Well, in that you are too late, my friend, for *I* have already challenged *you*."

"Not so fast, you puppy."

"Whom do you think to call a puppy?" cried Arthur, leaning his fists upon the table and glaring down at Sir Richard.

"You, you ass! By heaven, two can play at this game. If you go to see his lordship, I shall be right along with you. I shall ask him to second me."

"You cannot! I thought of him first!"

"Aye, it is the same with Charlotte. Because you thought to win her first, no one else may intervene. Well, we shall see how it goes. In fact, I am not about to wait for you. I am going right out this minute to call upon him."

"Very well, we shall leave it up to him. We shall both ask his favor and accept his decision. If you have done with your breakfast, we can go now."

"What, you are going with me in my carriage?" asked Sir Richard.

"As I have not one of my own, of course. It would look like the dickens if we each of us arrived separately, and me in a hackney coach!"

Sir Richard leaned back in his seat and stared at his guest, perplexed. "Arthur, you continue to amaze me. Does it not strike you that once we have broached the subject to his lordship, he will know damn well that we are on the outs with each other?"

"Very well, we shall go together but leave separately."

At which remark Sir Richard howled with laughter.

After Arthur had a chance to run over in his mind precisely what he had said, he grinned sheepishly. "It is only because you have got me beside myself with this business," he explained lamely.

"I begin to suspect that you were beside yourself from the day you were born, turnip wit!"

CHAPTER TWELVE

Later that same morning, at half-past eleven, Lord Faile, who had spent a miserable night tossing and turning whilst his heart and mind did battle with each other, was disturbed at his breakfast by callers.

He was attired in a dressing gown and had not shaved, having experienced an overwhelming desire for a cup of chocolate, immediately upon arising some twenty minutes previous.

His footman, when he came in to announce the callers, begged to be excused for his impertinence in intruding upon his lordship's morning, but he'd been led to believe that the business was a matter of life and death.

This did not appear to impress the marquis to any extent other than to elicit from him a groan followed by an inquiry as to the identity of his visitors. Upon being informed that they were Sir Richard Shadworth and Mr. Arthur Westley, Lord Faile frowned:

"Good God! I just spent a day in their company! Could they have not approached me on this business, whatever it is, at that time?"

The footman refused to incriminate himself by offering an opinion, and remained standing mutely by until his master saw fit to instruct him.

"Very well, if it is so hell-fired bloody important, they shall just have to put up with me as I am. Send 'em in to me."

As soon as the two gentlemen entered the breakfast room, Sir Richard declared, "My lord, I would not have intruded upon you at this ungodly hour for anything if it was *my* decision, but this erstwhile friend of mine was bound and determined upon it, and I could not dissuade him. Rather than allow him to make a complete ass of himself, I have come along to attempt, in any way I can, to ameliorate his obvious lack of breeding and consideration for others."

At once Arthur wheeled upon him: "You infernal blackguard, you never told me this was too early to make a call!"

Sir Richard, a superior smile upon his face, bent to his lordship and offered in pseudo-confidence, "The fellow is green from the country, my lord, although one would think that after a twelvemonth in the City, he would have learned him some manners."

"So it is not a matter of life and death, as you led my footman to believe," said Lord Faile.

"As a matter of fact, it is, my lord," said Arthur, "but it can wait upon a more convenient time if it pleases you."

His lordship cast a quizzical glance at Sir Richard, who shrugged in response and said, "He would insist upon this, my lord."

"Be seated, gentlemen. As long as you are here and do not take violent exception to my lack of toilet, we may as well discuss whatever it is you have come to discuss."

They did so and were served cups of steaming chocolate. While Sir Richard sipped at his, Arthur spoke out:

"My lord, I humbly request that you will act as my second in an affair of honor.

"Are you out of your skull, Westley? It is quite against His Majesty's laws. I mean to say, I do not think it ever was a legal practice, but now the peace officers take a very dim view of the matter and think nothing of hauling one into court. As your second, I should have to face my peers in the House of Lords, which I am not about to do."

"Now, will you be satisfied, you bumblebrain?" said Sir Richard.

Arthur sank back in disappointment, but replied, "Not a bit! I challenge you to a mill in Jackson's Academy. You have always claimed that I knocked you down because you were not prepared. Now you will have your chance to prove it. In the event that you are quite in error upon that score, you will, in the future, refrain from paying your attentions to Miss Lequesne."

"Is that what this is all about?" inquired Lord Faile. "You know, I was something puzzled yesterday that you, Westley, spent your time with Phoebe, whereas you, Shadworth, spent your time with Charlotte. I had been informed it was quite the other way about."

The conversation came hot and heavy after that, and it was some time before his lordship could comprehend the precise nature of the quarrel and bring his two acquaintances to a more reasoned temper:

"All right, gentlemen—all right! I do believe that we can do without the vituperation. First of all, if you will give me your attention and cease this pointless glaring at each other like two curs spoiling for a brawl, perhaps we can begin to untangle it."

They both murmured their apologies, and Lord Faile, satisfied that he had brought them to order, began to speak:

"It appears to me, from what you have been saying, that the simplest thing would be for you to exchange with each other. Is there any reason to object to this settling of the accounts between you?"

"Most assuredly, my lord!" exclaimed Arthur. "It is my intention to ask Charlotte's hand in marriage. Now do you ask Shadworth what *he* intends."

"You are seriously proposing to marry the girl?" asked Lord Faile. "I mean to say . . . well, now, I do not mean to say that at all. What I mean to say is that you are a gentleman, sir. I do not deny that Miss Lequesne is a beauty and carries herself exceedingly well, but . . . there is the theater in her background—the ballet, to be precise about it."

"I am well aware of that, my lord," replied Arthur staunchly, "yet she will be my *lady* wife when I have wed her," and he balled his fists and brought them crashing together with a force that made his lordship wince and Sir Richard look thoughtful.

"Hmmm," said his lordship, "that is clear enough. Well, Shadworth, what are *your* intentions regarding Miss Lequesne?"

"I do believe *I* shall marry the gel," he replied blandly.

"What did you say?" exploded Arthur.

"Are your ears stuffed? I said I should marry the gel."

"The devil you say!"

"The devil I *do* say! What, are you the only one to do the deed?"

"It is bloody queer you saying so now! You never said so before!"

"I have been thinking," said Sir Richard, by way of explanation.

"The age of miracles has not passed, I see," declared Arthur.

"Shut your impudent clack box or my mauler will do it for you!" threatened Sir Richard, raising a fist in Arthur's direction.

Arthur was not impressed. "I still call it queer. What has brought this passion upon you so suddenly?"

"I told you: I have been thinking. I do not imagine I shall ever find another female with so grand a seat upon a horse. That can be pretty important in my set."

"Great God in heaven! Is that any reason for marrying a female?"

"Of course not! Not by itself. I never claimed it was. Charlotte has a number of fine points I am taken with, but I am not about to explain 'em to *you*."

Lord Faile sat back and shrugged his shoulders. "It seems we are at point-non-plus, gentlemen. Since you neither one of you takes exception to the lady's choice of vocation, I am not sure what you ought to do about it—but a duel is out of the question, and I absolutely will not have it. There has got to be a better way out of this dilemma."

"I say that you ought to choose Phoebe," declared Sir Richard.

"When I wish a suggestion from you, sir, I shall make a request," returned Arthur, with his nose in the air.

"Now, look you, Westley, I am not trying to do you in the matter. I am quite serious and make the suggestion out of friendliness. You know damn well that Charlotte would be wasted on a farm as a farmer's wife. For all the time you spent with Phoebe out Fulham way, it appears to me that she would fit your plans a sight better than Charlotte. She is all full of that farming rubbish you are always spouting. Gad, the pair of you make a perfect bore!"

"But Phoebe is not a lady," protested Arthur rather weakly.

Lord Faile snorted. "What has that to say to anything? I know that Charlotte comes of gentle stock, but she has as much of the stage behind her as Phoebe. Actually, Shadworth's problem in that regard will be greater than yours. He has got to contend with London's accepting his lady, whereas you will have only the bumpkins of Leicestershire to contend with. It comes to the same thing at the best."

"Do you really think so?" asked Arthur, hoping to be convinced.

"It is my honest opinion," said Lord Faile firmly.

"Phoebe *is* a dear girl, you know. I mean to say, I do not object to her personally in the least, not at all."

"And she is not exactly cool to you, my friend," pointed out Sir Richard.

"I say, Dick, do you truly think so?" asked Arthur, grinning broadly now.

"I take it the matter is settled and it is now up to the ladies," said Lord Faile.

"Indeed, my lord, and I wish to offer you my deep thanks," said Arthur, rising and shaking hands with his lordship. "I am going right over to the Opera House and put it to her."

"Whoa, man, hold your horses! That is no way to go about this business," said Lord Faile.

"It is not?" asked Arthur. "Why, what do you suggest, my lord?"

"Egad, the way you go about it is *your* business. I just think you ought not to rush it, is all."

"I say!" exclaimed Sir Richard. "I have an idea. Arthur, let us take them out to Fulham again. I mean to say, it will be the most natural thing for Phoebe to stay with you and for Charlotte to go riding with me. Yes, that would make the business much easier, I do not doubt."

Arthur turned to his lordship for his approval.

Lord Faile nodded. "It sounds a perfect solution. Now, I pray you gentlemen will excuse me. I have my own matters to attend to."

The gentlemen, both of them now on the best of terms with each other and beginning to speak in glowing terms of their future prospects, took leave of his lordship and departed.

Once they were gone, Lord Faile fell back in his chair and his features underwent a drastic change. His usually calm and collected countenance was now the very picture of doubt and worry. "Damn!" he swore. "And I thought I had got it all worked out. What a pair they are—two bumblebrains!—and they have thrown me into confusion. I have all that thinking to do all over again. Blast! I swear I shall never have another dealing with a ballerina . . . er . . . not but one more—perhaps."

CHAPTER THIRTEEN

Phoebe and Arthur were grinning like a pair of loons as they held each other about the waist while Charlotte and Sir Richard rode into the paddock. So happy were they with themselves that, for the moment, they failed to notice how erect and cold was Charlotte in her saddle and how dogged and sulky was Sir Richard in his. It was impressed upon them, however, when Sir Richard went to assist Charlotte down from her seat and she waved him away with an imperious gesture, beckoning to one of the grooms to assist her instead, that the state of affairs between their friends was excessively frigid. Slowly their ecstatic smiles faded away, to be replaced by a look of concern. Arthur left Phoebe and went forward to speak with Sir Richard, while Charlotte came hurrying up to Phoebe, the icy look upon her face beginning to melt into tears as she said, "Dearest Phoebe, I pray you will accompany me back to the house. I have no wish to converse with *that* gentleman any further."

Phoebe cast a glance of inquiry at Arthur, who was frowning. He nodded to her and she led Charlotte away. Arthur turned to Sir Richard, who was leaning against his mount and mopping at his face with a handkerchief. There was a haunted look in his eyes as he swore softly under his breath.

"Dick, old man, you look like you have been knocked out of time. Did you and Charlotte have words?"

There was a look of disgust in Sir Richard's face as he snarled, "What does it look like? *You* seem to have done all right. It is as I always said: There is just no way to deal with a lady. See how easy it was for you to gain your way with Phoebe."

"I ought to deliver you a jawbreaker for that remark. I'll have you know that my Phoebe is every bit the lady, and God have mercy on any man who does not treat her so, for I shall not!"

"Oh, damnit, Arthur, you mistake my meaning! It all adds up to the fact that your Phoebe has her feet on the ground and knows a good offer when she receives one. I mean to say, she did accept you, did she not?"

"What does it look like?" retorted Arthur, turning all colors and grinning.

Sir Richard smiled at that and reached out. "Here's my hand on it, lad. My heartiest congratulations! I am sure she will make you an excellent wife, nothing like that cold fish of a Miss Lequesne."

"Dick, old man, I find it incredibly difficult to understand how she came to turn you down. I was sure that she had naught but good regard for you."

"Who can say what goes on in those high-nosed females' minds. What the devil has she got to be so high-nosed about, I should like to know? After all, what is she? Who is she? Nothing but a ballerina, beautiful as all get-out and as proud as a duchess. I have had my fill of her!"

"I say, about these sentiments—you did not in any

way give her to understand that you were condescending, did you?"

"What would you have me say? That *I* am aiming above my station? Certainly I took pains to show her that she would not be stepping *down* to me."

"You idiot! You stupid numskull! You out-and-out shatterbrain! Did you expect her to scrape and bow to you? Is that what you are asking of the lady who condescends to be your wife? That lady is to be Lady Shadworth, you noodle! She will rank with your mother, you ass! If this is how you feel about the matter, I should not marry her if I were you—and she would be a fool to accept you."

Sir Richard looked puzzled. "You are not going to tell me that that is anything like the manner with which you dealt with Phoebe, are you?"

A strained expression came to Arthur's face. "It is altogether different, Dick. Can't you see that Charlotte is another female entirely? I mean to say, just because Charlotte and Phoebe are females, it does not go to say that they are the same. You and I, we are not the same though we share one gender. In fact, if you come to think of it, by reason of our frames and height, we resemble each other far more closely than the girls do each other, yet you would never think to say that you and I are the same. Dick, you are in a sad case if you cannot tell one female from another and must treat with them all the same," ended Arthur, shaking his head.

"I never really thought about it before. I treated 'em all alike and had no complaint."

Arthur sneered. "I daresay! But you will have to change your ways now. It is something different to address the lady whom you wish to wed and some light-skirt who gives not a damn what you say to her so long as it is followed by a full purse."

"There's all that difference, is there? I mean to say,

you did not just go up to Phoebe and tell her to marry you?"

"Oh, but you are hopeless! Is that what you did with Charlotte, *command* her to wed the Grand Panjandrum Sir Richard Shadworth?"

Sir Richard merely stood with eyes cast down.

"Hmmm, I thought as much. You may be up to the nines with regard to the City, but I am far ahead of you when it comes to the Sex, my friend. Tell me, Dick, do you truly have a wish to wed Charlotte? You have always made a great noise about how difficult the ladies were. Before you speak, remember that Charlotte is a lady, and that may be deal more than you care to bargain for."

This time Sir Richard sighed. "I venture to say that I ought to have spent more time in the company of ladies. Yes, I do believe I should like to have Charlotte for wife. Until this afternoon's ride, we got along famously. I say, old man, have I lost my chance with her?"

"I do not know. The only way you will find that out is to try your luck with her again."

"Yes, but how do I go about it?"

"Beg her, plead with her, go down upon your knees to her. You might even try a tear or two."

"What, you expect me to weep like a forlorn maiden? What the devil do you think I am!" exclaimed Sir Richard angrily.

"I think you are a loon. If you had done it right in the first place, you would not now be having to ask my advice," retorted Arthur.

"I bloody well am *not* asking your advice. By heaven, I shall do this my way and she will wed me whatever she thinks!" shouted Sir Richard, stalking off to the house.

Nancy was strolling about the apartment like a lost soul. She was deep in a brown study. Actually, she was so very melancholy, it was more a blue mood she was in. There had been a change in Tony this evening. Not only had he not been any fun; he seemed to have been bored with her, and this frightened her.

There was always the remembrance of how he had treated Fleurette, the prima ballerina of the Opera. She never did know precisely why Tony had taken up with her, a milliner's assistant, but had always suspected that he wished to make her the successor to Fleurette. If she had not always the picture of Fleurette falling out of the marquis's regard, she might have succumbed, for she had not a doubt in the world that she was in love with Tony. But all she could envision was the horror of his casting her out when he had had enough of her and sending her packing, just as he had done with Fleurette.

In Fleurette's case, it was no great tragedy. The Frenchwoman had shrugged the affair off and taken up with another protector without the least hesitation. For Nancy, that could never be. She would be completely crushed even as she sensed she was about to be. Tony had made it quite plain that he wanted her and had been marvelously patient with her. Now she could see that his patience was coming to an end and, as she could not bring herself to share Fleurette's fate, her time with Tony was running out.

Oh, she wished the girls would return home! She needed desperately to talk it all out, and they would be quite sympathetic. She knew that in their hearts they had never wished for her the destiny of all ballerinas and had, when they'd first shared the garret, gone to great pains to keep her out of the sight of the lizards in the lobby. Surely now they would have some kind word for her.

Of one thing she was certain: Once Tony had done with her, she could no longer stay on at the Opera. For all the great success she was enjoying, it would be more than she could bear to see Tony with some other female of the theater. It would be bad enough when he took a lady to be his marquise, but, as that was inevitable, she must resign herself to it. To lose Tony to another dancer, however—that would be too much!

Yes, she would have to leave the Opera. In fact, she would have to leave London. No, England was too small. Under those circumstances, she would have to go across the Channel to France. Ah, France! Yes, Signor Bouquin would tell her whom to see in Paris. Surely she was competent enough to perform with the Ballet Française. After all, she could dance *en pointe,* and she knew, from Signor Bouquin's remarks, that the only other ballerina to make a name for herself *sur les pointes* was Mademoiselle Taglioni, and she was in Denmark. Yes, she would go to France.

Suddenly she discovered that she was weary of walking aimlessly about and she sat herself down. Now she would think of how she would tell Tony and of what he would say to it. Her version of the parting scene was so very sad. It made her weep.

Nancy was brought abruptly back to the present by the sounds of Charlotte and Phoebe returning home. It was a very noisy entrance she heard. The girls must have been in the highest spirits, for much laughter punctuated their chattering. She got up quickly and went out to them.

"Nancy, are you back so soon?" exclaimed Charlotte. "Oh, I would have had you meet Sir Richard if I had known. Ah, little one, we have got the most *marvelous* news."

Nancy smiled uncertainly as she asked, "What is it?"

"Come, child, this cannot wait," replied Charlotte, taking her by the hand and leading her back to the drawing room. When they'd all sat down, she announced, "My dear, in a little while, for the best of reasons, this friendly trio of ours is going to break up."

"Wh-why ever should it?" asked Nancy.

Phoebe spoke up: "Oh, Charlotte, that is never the way! Nancy, pet, Charlotte and I, we each of us have been asked to wed and we have accepted."

For a moment Nancy was not sure she understood. She raised a finger and pointed, first at Phoebe and then at Charlotte. "The both of you?"

"The both of us, my dear. Arthur Westley for me and Sir Richard Shadworth for Charlotte, although he almost didn't. It all went off very well, quite beyond our wildest dreams. Just think of it: I am going to be a Leicestershire lady!"

Nancy could only stare at the pair of them, then a bright smile came to her lips, after a bit of effort, while her heart felt like lead. All she could think of was that the end had truly come. Without Charlotte's and Phoebe's affection for her refuge, she surely must depart the country. She could never stay by herself. Masking her unhappiness, she asked joyfully, "How did it come about? You must tell me everything!"

"Well, if you know Arthur, you know that he is not at all a forward sort of gentleman, and so, when we were in the midst of rows upon rows of corn, he opened upon the subject in such a fiddle-footed manner, I was led completely up the garden path. I was sure it was carte blanche he was asking me to accept. If that was the best offer I could get from him, I was not about to reject it and so I said yes.

"His very next words, under the circumstances, quite shocked me, and you know that I am not easily startled: 'When can we do it? I am in a bit of a hurry to get back to Leicestershire, you know.' "

Phoebe began to laugh so hard she had to place her hand upon her ample bosom to keep from bursting.

"I replied," she went on, " 'Since we neither of us have our own lodgings, it is going to take a bit of time, or do you have some place in mind?' He replied, 'But of course, we shall go home to Leicestershire. I see no difficulty, as I am sure I can procure a special license and we shall be man and wife before the week is out.'

"I do not know how long I stood frozen to the spot with shock. I could not believe he had said what he had. I managed to say, 'You would wed me?' And he cried, 'What in bloody hell do you think I am talking about?' So I told him, and he turned the prettiest pink you ever did see, even as he roared with laughter. I pummeled him a bit for it and he pummeled me a bit and that was *that* as far as anyone else is concerned," Phoebe ended with a salacious grin.

"How perfectly marvelous!" cried Nancy, jumping up and clapping her hands together. She ran to Phoebe and gave her a great hug. "When is it to be?"

"Oh, who knows? Arthur will be out seeking the license tomorrow—but wait! Let me tell you what happened to Charlotte. I swear I thought that she and Sir Richard would never speak to each other again."

"Now, Phoebe, you make me regret that I told you anything at all."

"Surely you cannot object to Nancy's knowing. Little one, it was like this——"

"If it is to be told, *I* shall do the telling, Phoebe," said Charlotte indignantly. "I fear to hear what *you* would make of it. Nancy, I pray you will not repeat a word of this. Heaven knows how embarrassed Richard is over the business. You see, he just did not understand."

"Good heavens, what *did* happen? You look to be as much in alt as Phoebe. He did *offer,* did he not?"

"Well, of course he did!" exclaimed Charlotte with a toss of her head. "In fact, I refused him at the first."

"Oh, you didn't!" exclaimed Nancy.

"She most certainly did, I can vouch for it. I saw

Sir Richard's face and it was as black as thunder," Phobe attested.

"Phoebe, it is my story and I shall tell it, *if* you will allow me."

Phoebe chortled and dropped back into her seat. "Go on, Lady Shadworth," said she with a wave of her hand. "I shan't say another word."

Charlotte looked at her with a troubled expression. "I say, my dear, you will not embarrass me when I introduce you to Sir Richard's friends, will you?"

"Oh, go on! What has Phoebe Bell of Billingsgate to do with the likes of Lady Charlotte?"

"Now, Phoebe Bell, you hearken to me," replied Charlotte, shaking a finger at her friend. "You will be Mrs. Arthur Westley, the wife of a Leicester gentleman who is bosom beau to Sir Richard. There will be no more of Billingsgate and ballet for you, my girl, and you had better know it. By heaven, if Arthur will not teach you, I shall!"

Phoebe's smile did not fade, but she did look thoughtful. "It is like a dream. I think he truly loves me. He told me how he had been dangling after you, Charlotte, because he had never got to know me, only my reputation." She heaved a great sigh of satisfaction and waved her hand again. "Go on, my lady. The little one is all ears, and I would not mind hearing it again."

Charlotte gave her a disdainful glance and proceeded: "What happened was that while we were out riding, we came to a shaded pond and Sir Richard suggested that we dismount and rest the horses. We did so and sat us down in the shade of a great tree. Without any ceremony, out of a clear blue sky, he stated flatly that he had decided to wed me. Just like that!

"I was not to have a thing to say about it. I told him

very plainly that if this was his way of making an of-fer, I was not about to have any.

"He became quite angry at that and demanded to know who I thought I was, refusing him like that. I was about to tell him, but he followed his demand with the statement that he obviously was in grave error about me and withdrew whatever it was he had said.

"I immediately arose and said that I asked nothing of him except his assistance to regain my seat, as side saddles were never designed for easy mounting. When he'd assisted me, I thanked him and started back.

"For a moment, I was sure that all was lost, because he watched me ride off without making a move to follow. I tell you I could have cried right there and then, but I thought it would be better not to let him catch sight of my tears and I urged my horse on.

Charlotte smiled as she went on: "No, all was not yet lost, for he came racing after me. Once he'd gained my side, I could feel him staring at me—or glaring, rather—but I took no notice and continued on. That was how we came back to the paddock.

"Well, I could see at a glance that Phoebe had been a deal more fortunate than I, and I hurried her off to the house so that we could talk. Some twenty minutes later, there came a thunderous rapping on the door of the dressing chamber where we were sitting, and Phoebe went to answer it. Of course, I knew it was Richard, and Phoebe did, too. When she opened the door, he immediately wished her well, explaining that she was getting a very fine gentleman, the very finest—for a farmer, he *would* have to add—and then asked permission to speak with me in private.

"Phoebe, like the dear girl she is, tripped out, and in he came, his face all twisted with anger, I thought. I stood up immediately and was about to tell him it was no use, but before I could get the words out of my mouth, to my astonishment, he sank down upon one knee and looked up at me with the strangest expression, saying, 'I say, I am not used to asking for a lady's hand. Is this something more like what you require?' "

Charlotte paused and looked off into the distance, her cheeks flaming, a repressed little smile upon her lips.

"Then what happened?" inquired Nancy eagerly.

Charlotte let out a little laugh. "How could I resist him after that? Things went very well from that point on, very well indeed. . . ." Her voice trailed off into silence.

"Oh, Charlotte, I am so happy for you, for the both of you! I wish you every joy!" cried Nancy, and went to hug her, too, with tears streaming down her cheeks. As both Charlotte and Phoebe also had moist eyes, they could not know that Nancy was crying as much for her own sadness as for their new-found happiness.

In another part of the City, in a great house situated in Park Lane, the marquis of Faile discovered he had two callers, and the hour was quite late for that sort of thing. In fact, he had had a most trying day and had been on the verge of retiring, not to sleep so much as to continue to think over the problem that seemed to have no reasonable solution for him.

He had doffed his coat and was in his shirt sleeves when his footman came to inform him that Sir Richard Shadworth and Mr. Arthur Westley wished to have a word with him, adding, "And, my Lord, if you will permit me to observe, the gentlemen are a few sheets to the wind, I am sure."

Lord Faile placed one hand on his hip and the other upon his troubled brow. "If it is not one thing, it is another. I think they presume upon our acquaintance, which is of the slightest, to call upon me at such an hour. I venture to say it can only be that they are pot-valiant at the moment, and it would but cause a scene if I were to refuse them. Very well—bring them to me and let us get it over with."

When the gentlemen were conducted into his presence, he could see that they were in truth in high spirits, but that something other than spirituous liquors was the cause.

"My dear Faile, congratulations are in order, old chap," said Sir Richard, approaching him with his hand thrust forward, "and it is you we have to thank for our good fortune."

Replied Lord Faile, "Then congratulations indeed, Sir Richard, but I am sure I could be more sincere in my wishes if I understood the occasion for them."

"Why, we are to be wed! You it was who suggested that change-about, and it was precisely what we both of us wanted—our ladies, too, it appears."

Lord Faile looked staggered. He fell back into a chair and motioned Sir Richard and Arthur to be seated. "You . . . you are going to marry them—the ladies, I mean?"

"Yes, of course. Actually, I suppose it was Arthur's idea at first, but you know that sort of thing can be rather catching, especially when it is my lady Charlotte who is in the offing."

Although his lordship looked a little pale, he nodded and smiled. "Indeed, gentlemen, my heartfelt good wishes attend you."

"I am so pleased to hear you say so, for we have come to beg a boon of you for the sake of friendship."

Lord Faile frowned and blinked. "A boon?"

"Aye," said Arthur with a rush. "Insomuch as you are the friend of their dear friend—our ladies, I mean —Miss Faulconer, Dick and I decided it would be perfectly smashing, did we not, Dick?"

"We did, my lord. It came about because if I was to be best man to Arthur and he was to be best man to me, then a bit of a poser arose as to the precedents involved, don't you see. It would hardly be proper for us to be groom and best man at a double wedding that was our own, and then the question came up, which of us was to wed first? And that was only between ourselves. It could have turned into a Roman holiday if we brought the ladies into it."

"Er . . . I begin to see the problem," said the marquis uncertainly.

"Ah, then it makes it so much easier to ask you, my lord, to condescend to be to each of us our chief friend, or best man, as they would have it these days north of the border."

"What, me?" exclaimed his lordship, plainly startled.

"But of course. Who better? After all, it was you who managed to straighten the business out—and, too, I wish to point out how much it would mean to our ladies if his lordship, the Marquis of Faile, gave his blessing. I mean to say, it would go far to ameliorating the business of the ballet, don't you see. That is bound to be something for people to stick at, and it would be a great favor to us if you could put any reservations to rest on that score. Certainly *you* do not find our choice of brides exceptional, do you?"

"Why . . . ah, no. Of course I do *not!*" Lord Faile seemed to be attempting to compensate for his slight hesitation by overstresing his concordance.

"Excellent, my lord!" cried Arthur. "Then you'll do it!"

"Yes. Yes, of course. It will be a distinct pleasure to stand up with the both of you. Now, gentlemen, it is late and I do have some business to attend to before I retire."

After they had departed, Lord Faile got down to the business he had referred to. It called for no more effort than that of sitting down in an easy chair and

pondering hard well into the late hours of the night,
Indeed, it was almost daybreak before he had had
enough. He was not sure he had arrived at any conclusion, but he was too tired to go on. He went to bed
and slept till well past noon.

CHAPTER FOURTEEN

Nancy was perched on a stool, stage right, regarding with a discontent Signor Bouquin's tantrum. He had just been informed that two of his ladies of the corps had deserted him in his hour of need, and for such a poor excuse as having to be wed. Mr. Coates was also looking glum and had very little to add to the ballet master's long, complaining tirade. The loss of La Belle Bell was bound to be reflected as a substantial decrease in the house's take, and he would be hard put to find another such statuesque beauty.

Signor Bouquin was not at all concerned for the loss of Phoebe; he was infuriated over the fact that Charlotte's leaving the company made a shambles of the ensemble. It was not that she was such a marvelous performer—he considered her merely competent— but that he could no longer divide his ensemble into two equal ranks of eight ballerinas each, a usage that bordered upon the sacred with him. That the ranks should be equal and exactly comprised of eight ladies was as the breath of life to him, a fact well known to the entire company. What his tirade was going to accomplish, no one of the company could imagine. They were too filled with envy over the good fortune of their late fellow performers. Of course, it was not for the fact of their forthcoming marriages, but rather for the unexceptional elevation these connections would bring to them. Why, one of them, Charlotte Lequesne, was reaching as high as the lesser nobility, no mean feat for a ballerina.

Nancy sighed with a resignation that masked her impatience with the ballet master. Obviously this was no time to broach the topic of her prospects with the Opera in Paris with him. If he had suspected that she, too, was about to desert the glorious ranks of the English Opera, *his* ballet company, he would be fit to be tied down and a keeper called. She would have to wait for a more propitious moment. In the meantime, it was growing late, and if Signor Bouquin saw fit not to proceed with the rehearsal, this would be a day of very little accomplishment—and it certainly appeared that that was how it would be.

Now Mr. Coates was making an attempt to soothe Signor Bouquin. He was forced to agree that they had been served a pretty poor turn by the two ladies in question, but one could hardly blame them for accepting such promising opportunities. *"C'est la vie,* signor. You have got to face it, old chap. It is all a part of the business, you see."

Signor Bouquin closed his mouth tightly and regarded the theater manager with disdain. Then he said, "To me, Bouquin, you say *'C'est la vie'?"*

"My dear fellow, I am just trying to get you to put a good face on it. It is done, and all that is left to us is to apply ourselves to remedying the situation. Do not worry! I will find you another girl. It will not be all that difficult to find a replacement for Miss Lequesne. She was not the first ballerina, nor need she be the last."

"You will do this thing *tout de suite?*"

"Absolutely! Never doubt it. I understand how much it means to you."

Signor Bouquin nodded and slowly folded his arms across his chest. *"Bien,* then I begin rehearsals when you have brought to me the replacement. Until then, no more rehearsals." He nodded again and stalked off the stage.

Mr. Coates swore under his breath. Then he turned and glared at the company, assembled in various poses about the stage. "All of you are dismissed for the day —but wait! Do not rush off. If you know of any promising young lady with an eye for a place with us, I implore you to bring her to my attention. We are quite at a loss for the moment and will be straightaway in hot water if we cannot get these rehearsals started up again. Believe me, ladies and gentlemen, your livelihood depends upon filling this gap in our ranks just as does mine. I bid you think on it and good night!"

Nancy sighed again and got off her stool. Even as she descended to the little cubbyhole that was her own personal dressing room, she was very much aware of the absence of Charlotte and Phoebe. They had been such staunch supporters and enthusiastic friends that she was bound to miss them. And the loss verged on the painful, because there was no one else in the company who could take their place with her. She was, after all, the star of the ballet, ranking with Fleurette, the prima ballerina, and as she also enjoyed the regard of the Marquis of Faile, the other ballerinas had set a distance between themselves and her, in much the same fashion as the citizenry and the nobility are set apart from each other. The only reason that Charlotte and Phoebe had not been drawn away from her was the fact they had been roommates who had started in the company at the very same time with her.

Now that the fate of those ladies was sealed in so

happy a manner, there was no question but that Nancy could never find other friends to take their place. It was more than a suspicion with her that their vows of undying friendship were not to be relied upon. They were removing themselves from the socially unacceptable world of the theater to the high realms of genteel society, so that a connection with a ballerina, however notable, would not sit well with the people of the new circles in which they would be moving. France, even Italy, if necessary, must be her destination, and she must inform Tony at once—if she could but get to see him.

She finished dressing and prepared to leave the theater. She looked about her for a bit, trying to imagine how it would be when she came to look upon it for the last time. She was sure it would be a very painful moment. It was hurting her deep inside just to contemplate it.

Once outside, she decided to walk home instead of taking a hackney coach to the apartment, her usual practice since she had come into a handsome salary. She was in no particular hurry to have to face the great joy of her friends, who had undoubtedly been out to the shops buying up all of London so that they might make a respectable appearance at their forthcoming nuptials.

She never reached the door to the great house in which her apartment was situated. As she neared it, a hand upon her arm brought her round, face to face with the Marquis of Faile.

She smiled up at him. "Tony, what a surprise! I had hoped you would call."

"Where the devil have you been? I have been sitting in my carriage for an hour waiting for you. I know that there is not that much doing at the Opera House at the moment to have delayed you. I have been out of my mind with worry to the extent that I almost braved the great joys that must be flooding your rooms to make inquiries of the brides-to-be as to your possible whereabouts."

Her smile faded. "Are you not happy for them, my lord?" she asked.

"Of course, but at the moment I have some matters of my own to attend to and have not the stomach to be all bright and cheery, as they are bound to expect. Come, I have a wish to speak with you."

Nancy could see that Tony was irked about something and she was feeling very blue that he should look upon the happiness of her friends so coldly. "My lord, I would have a word with you, too. Let us go up and talk together."

"Up there? No, I have a better idea. It has been a very long time since you joined me for supper under my own roof. It would be my pleasure if you would agree to sup with me this night."

Nancy thought that would not do at all. She looked intently at him, trying to fathom what he had in mind, and because she could not be sure, she shook her head. "No, my lord, I beg to refuse your kind suggestion. Perhaps there is some other place."

"There is no other place for what I would say to you. Come, I shall not accept a refusal." Gently but firmly he took her by the arm and led her over to his carriage at the curb, assisted her into it, signaled to the coachman, and sat down beside her.

As the carriage started off, Nancy turned to him and said, "This is not fair of you, my lord. I . . . I am not at ease in Faile House."

"How do you know that? You have been there only one or two times."

"It is a fact, my lord, and I am telling you so."

Tony turned to look sharply at her. "Are you serious? I had always hoped you liked the place and would come, eventually, to spend a great deal of time there."

Bitterness welled up in Nancy and she replied, "I must consider myself honored above many others, I suppose. I never heard that Fleurette was given that privilege."

"I say, you seem to be in something of a pet tonight. I wish you would leave Fleurette out of it and——"

"Gladly, my lord, and I do not think the carriage need continue on. I can say what I have to say here and now. It is simply this: I shall not be needing your apartment for much longer. I am off to France to the French Opéra."

"The devil you say! I shall never allow it! You are doing very well right here in England and I would——"

"My lord, it is no use, I have quite made up my mind. I have heard it said that the ballet in France is ever so much finer than ours. I think it would enhance my prestige if I could succeed over there as I have succeeded here."

"And what if you should fail? I know for a fact that the French are quite excellent. Only the Italians are better, and these days not by very much."

Nancy shrugged. "If it should happen that way, I hope that I shall be able to return."

"Does the ballet mean so much to you?" he asked, a note of dismay in his voice.

"It means everything to me, my lord. I . . . I have nothing else."

"Nancy, what has come over you? I should think that you would be sharing the mood of your friends— but wait! Have you told them what you have just told me?"

Nancy looked down and shook her head.

"I thought as much. It is a rather sudden decision on your part, is it not?"

Nancy shrugged and looked out of the window.

"What in blazes is bedeviling you, girl? This is definitely not the Nancy I know."

"You have my heartfelt regrets, my lord."

"Now you are making it close to impossible to even talk with you."

"My lord, I have said what I have to say and I pray you will see that there is no good purpose to continuing on. If you will have the carriage halted, I shall find my own way home."

"Damme! But you are up in the trees about something, aren't you? I say, has anyone at the theater been harsh with you? I shall soon put a stop to it—— Ah, we have arrived," he said as the carriage drew to a stop before the house in Park Lane.

"Tony, please allow me to depart!" Nancy pleaded, placing a hand on his arm.

"In a minute if I understood this strange mood that has taken hold of you. Nancy, what is it?"

"It is only that I am not overjoyed at having to leave England."

"That is precisely what I do not understand. Why do you *have* to leave England? While you are here, you enjoy my protection—you know that—and I have no intention of withdrawing it from you—ever."

Nancy was beginning to weep. She felt very helpless. If Tony had been something less than a marquis, perhaps she might have tried to explain some part of her feelings in the matter. But he was so far above her. Charlotte had gained the affection of a knight, and she was already a lady. What a monstrous hope, what an impertinence for her, a former shopgirl, to say to the Marquis of Faile what was in her heart. It was amazing enough that she could address him by his first name!

The tears were the last straw. Exasperated, Tony declared, "Now that you have succeeded in making me feel a positive monster, I am bound to get to the bottom of this business, young lady! No, I shall not permit you to leave. We are going in together and we are going to sit down together and we are going to talk together until it is very clear to me what I have done that is so awful."

"Oh, Tony, you do not understand!" she wailed, falling on his breast and clinging to him.

"Call me slow top then, my pet, but I am not at all convinced that your love for the dance is so all-fired passionate that you must seek out the ends of the earth to satisfy it. Come along, now. Perhaps you have been working too hard. I shall have a talk with that slave driver of a Bouquin on the morrow."

Nancy allowed herself to be conducted into the house, where Tony gave her a little push and said, "Go and refresh yourself. Rest, if you wish, and then come down to me in the small dining room. I will await you there."

Nancy did as she was bid—that is, she repaired the ravages of tears and did some things to her hair, then sat down for a bit, not to rest but to regain her composure. She was ashamed of herself for having broken down like a little girl crying for the moon—and that was precisely the way it was with her. Tony was so close and yet so unattainable. The truly awful thing that was becoming clear to her was the fact that it was so very easy to say that she was leaving the country as compared with doing the deed itself. She had the gravest doubt that she could put so much distance between herself and Tony of her own free will. Now, when she felt so very vulnerable to him and so much in need of his love, rather than of the kind affection with which he had always regarded her, she was being forced to spend an evening with him alone and in his house. The apprehension that was in her over the prospect was not due to anything Tony might initiate but to the fact that, in her desperate wish for his love, she might betray herself into that futureless future that she so much dreaded and truly earn the epithet "light-skirt."

When she came into the dining room, she was smiling. Tony rose and smiled back in relief, assisting her to a chair.

As he sat down, he said, "I have asked Gaston to be particularly at pains and do himself proud tonight —nothing heavy to stultify our conversation but light and refreshing to stimulate it."

"It is very kind of you, Tony."

"You are not angry with me, then?"

"I could never be angry with you, Tony."

"I hope that is true, for I am going to try to talk you out of your partiality for the ballet."

Nancy frowned. "It is a hopeless task for you to undertake. There is nothing I would rather do, nor is there anything else that I *can* do to earn my living."

"I wish you would not keep saying that. It most certainly is not the only thing that you can do, dammit! Not every female is bound to become a ballet dancer. You have only to look about you to see that there are other things in life besides dancing."

"Tony, what is all this in aid of? What would you have me do? Why are you all of a sudden set against my vocation? It will not change the fact that I am in love with you, which fact you find so distasteful. Whatever affection you bore me has cooled to the point that you are spending less and less time with me. I regret that I ever told you. Why do you continue, then? Is it for appearance's sake that you maintain a pretended interest in me? If so, it makes little sense."

"If that were so, it would make no sense at all. I do not pretend with you, and that you have declared your love to me is a delight; but it has presented me with a problem I had never encountered before, and I had to take some time to think about it. After all, you are a ballerina, risen from the ranks of the shopgirls, and I am a marquis. That is bound to call for serious contemplation."

Nancy shook her head in perplexity. "I am not asking for marriage, Tony. I wish it were possible that you could think of me as a wife to you, but I know my place and there is no changing the fact. And now that I am about to lose my only true friends, you must realize I cannot stay on with the company. You have already rejected me——"

"That is not true! It was merely that I had to think about it."

"Exactly what was there for you to think about? I do not understand. Did you have to think about Fleurette? Do you find something lacking in me that you found in her? Why, then, do you not go to her? I am sure that she would throw Lord Arliss over for you in a moment."

"You little nitwit! Yes, there is a difference in my thinking as between you and Fleurette. I was never in love with her as I am with you, and that was precisely my problem. I was never put to the trouble of having to consider how it would be if *Fleurette* were to become the Marquise of Faile."

Nancy stared at Tony as though she were stricken. "Th-that is your problem?" she asked incredulously.

"Yes!" he snapped.

"Th-then you are in love with me?" she said breathlessly.

"Yes!" he snapped.

"Oh, Tony! There is no problem!" she cried, and held out her arms to him.

He went to her, lifted her from the chair, and kissed her with an intensity that blanketed all Nancy's senses in a glorious cloud of pure gold, agleam with a happiness that was at once peaceful and yet passionate. Overall, there was the tremendous feeling of Tony's strength as he held her close to him, a protection, and a demand she had no wish to deny.

"My sweet little one, there *was* a problem," he whispered.

"Of course there was!" she chortled, leaning back in his arms so she could peer into his eyes. "You did not love me! Tony, when did you know?"

"You are still a ninny. I loved you from the start. What man in his right senses would give carte blanche to a lovely young thing and demand nothing in return?"

Nancy looked thoughtful. "Yes, I did wonder about that," she said, looking very serious.

Tony thought that look an excellent excuse to bestow another kiss, which he did without debating the matter.

There was a little air of impatience about Nancy as she broke away from his lips and demanded, "But if that was so, why did you reject me then and not now?"

"Then I did not know how to deal with it. Now I do —and it was those two noodles, Shadworth and Westley, who showed me the way."

"Sir Richard and Arthur? You told them about us?"

"No, of course I did not. It was just something that they requested of me that dropped the scales from my eyes."

"Then I have them to thank for my happiness?"

"In a manner of speaking, yes, but I would not mention it to them; it would only serve to confuse them both."

"I am sure I do not understand it at all."

"This is all you have got to understand, pet," he said vehemently, and kissed her again.

Nancy sighed with contentment. "Now I have got everything: I have your love and I have my success. I think I shall give a most excellent performance. I shall be so light upon my feet, all London will marvel."

"That they will not! You shall never appear upon a stage in public again, little one. I shall send round to Coates in the morning and inform him not to expect you back."

At that, Nancy pulled away from him and exclaimed, "Oh, Tony, no! You cannot ask that of me! You never demanded as much of Fleurette!"

"Don't you understand? I never asked Fleurette to be my marquise, either."

"Y-you would w-*wed* m-me? Me a marquise?" She stopped and stared at him. "Tony, you are quite mad. Whoever heard of a marquis marrying a shopgirl? You cannot be serious!"

"Then you had better resign yourself to having to wed a frivolous, mad marquis, little one, for that is what is going to happen."

"But that is unheard of. Tony, you will disgrace yourself, and I shall be the cause of it. Truly, Tony, it is not necessary."

He cocked a wry eye at her and replied, "You do not wish to be a marquise?"

"That is not the point. I would give anything if I could be *your* marquise, but it just is not done. Look at Charlotte. She is a gentlewoman and all she has got is a knight. I am not even of gentle birth."

"I was aware of that and that was the problem. But, as I have said, it is no longer."

"I do not see how you can say that. Nothing will change my origins. Even Charlotte will not have it very easy. There will always be the ballet in the background. With me, it is even worse, for my name has been plastered all over London. Everyone will know."

"I daresay that it might interfere with your being presented at Court for a bit, and I shall have the very devil of a time arranging for vouchers from Almack's for you, but if you behave like a very proper marquise, in time all will be forgiven and you will have your acceptance into the highest society. Needless to say, I shall look with extreme distaste upon anyone who dares to give you the cut direct."

"But, Tony——"

"Enough of these protestations or I shall begin to believe that I do not mean all that much to you."

Nancy laughed. "What nonsense!" she exclaimed, and kissed him to prove the validity of her observation. Then a sigh escaped her lips.

"It would appear, then, that I am no longer to dance."

"If it would please you, my lady, you could always dance for me."

"Yes, I should like that very much. When shall we be wed?"

"As soon as I can procure a special license—the day after tomorrow, I should imagine. It will be as long a wait as I can stand, my pet."

"Why, we shall be married before Charlotte and Phoebe are! What a surprise that will be."

"Which reminds me, we shall have to postpone the wedding trip for a bit. I promised to stand up with Shadworth and Westley. It will lend an air of approval to their nuptials. I hope you do not mind."

Nancy, for answer, threw her arms about him. "Oh, that is so very kind of you! It will do so much for Charlotte and Phoebe to have you as best man for their grooms. I do love you, Tony! You are so considerate." She kissed him warmly.

"Indeed. But think of how much it will do for you, my pet, to have me for *groom*. That was my solution, you see. If my presence could lend such approval to their unions, how much must it do for my own. I think I am being awfully considerate to you, don't you agree?"

Under the sweet barrage of her appreciation, further conversation was impossible.

When the news reached Signor Bouquin that the only toe dancer England could boast was retiring from her profession to wed the Marquis of Faile, he broke down and cried in the sight of the entire company.

REGENCY ROMANCES

BY MAGGIE GLADSTONE

Delightful Period Romances for your Reading Pleasure

BETTY HALE HYATT
___16674 **ANNA'S STORY** $1.95

SHEILA HOLLAND
___16464 **MAIDEN CASTLE** $1.50
___16479 **DANCING HILL** $1.50
___16535 **SHADOWS AT DAWN** $1.75
___16589 **THE NOTORIOUS** $1.75
       GENTLEMAN
___16635 **THE MERCHANT'S DAUGHTER** $1.95

PAULA ALLARDYCE
___16500 **THE ROGUE'S LADY** $1.50
___16568 **THE REBEL LOVER** $1.75
___16607 **THE VIXEN'S REVENGE** $1.95
___16686 **MY DEAR MISS EMMA** $1.95

JEAN RAYNES
___16519 **LEGACY OF THE WOLF** $1.50

DAWN LINDSEY
___16578 **DUCHESS OF VIDAL** $1.75

LILLIAN CHEATHAM
___16596 **THE SECRET OF SARAMOUNT** $1.75

MARJORIE SHOEBRIDGE
___16714 **A WREATH OF ORCHIDS** $1.95
